By: Stanley L. Battle

THE SON OF SCARFACE

MOCY PUBLISHING
WWW.MOCYPUBLISHING.COM

Detroit, Michigan

Printed by CreateSpace, An Amazon.com Company

The Son of Scarface

ISBN 978-1-940831-15-2

Published by Mocy Publishing, LLC.
Website: www.mocypublishing.com
Email: info@mocypublishing.com

The Son of Scarface

Preface

The Son of Scarface is based on what America has been waiting on for years; a part two to the film Scarface.

When you thought a father had no way of returning, his legend lives on through his son.

You are in for action, some drama, comedy, romance, and suspense.

If you thought the father was cold-blooded, low-down, dangerous, and full of lust for all the money in the world, wait until you meet "The Son of Scarface" face to face as your eyes venture through this book.

So kick back and relax, but do fasten your seatbelt as "The Son of Scarface" takes your mind on a cruise you'll never want to end.

When the son hollers at his prey he hollers in a mean kind of way!

Dedication

This book is dedicated to the inspiration of my soul. A woman who has been loving and supportive throughout the tough times in my life. I love you with all of my heart!

My mother,
Ms. Carolyn Malone

October 1, 1962

It was the 1st day of October 1962. After leaving Antonio, Gena moved to Detroit. It was the drug habit that Gena possessed that separated her and the dark hair Italian-Antonio Montero.

Antonio was very much in love with Gena even after being aware of her uncontrollable drug addiction.

He wanted so much for Gena to bear him a child; he desired a son more than anything. Even now as she stands gazing out of her window thinking of the past that she and her deceased husband shared together with tears running down her face onto her powered blue blouse. It was drenched as if she was just getting out of the shower, but thoughts continued to run through her mind.

"Only if Antonio was still alive and he could see his child being born. I know he wanted a boy so badly."

Deep in her heart she wanted to have a boy, his son. She had only a few months to go then the whole world would know.

"Oh how happy I will be if it's a boy," she kept thinking to herself as she took her seat saying out loud, "God please allow me to have a normal child. I hope the drugs I used to use don't have any affects on my baby. If I have a girl I'll name her Star, and if I have a boy I'm not sure what I would name him probably after his dead father. Oh…. I could hear me now calling his name come in the house Antonio."

Just the thought of her having a son would induce excitement in her as she continued imagining to herself.

"It's kind of difficult being in a rehabilitation center and pregnant at the same time, but with the Lord's help and the counselors behind me I can do it! No, no, no, I'm gonna do it especially if I want to have a healthy, normal baby. It is so important for me to have his baby. I'm my past actions I never saw myself feeling or thinking like this, but now I'm so damn glad to be at this center. The staff members here are so kind to me."

Gena was somewhat delighted that she had met a guy at the center that displayed he was interested in her. She thought he was a very nice guy and she had somewhat liked the sound of his name, "Shawn Bomoski."

Shawn had dark brown hair, pretty light brown eyes, and he was six feet even. Gena thought he was a very handsome man.

Shawn would often bring her a bouquet of roses in hopes that it would enlighten her day. He had even told her that he'd like to be part of her life.

She felt that Shawn was a very bright person, but at the same time she did not care to have a relationship with anyone.

"I haven't completely gotten over Antonio and God knows I don't need that type of situation again. Who knows, after the baby is born I might settle down and get remarried again, but right now I don't see that happening in the near future. Besides, Shawn's career as a doctor can never measure up to the lifestyle I'm use to living. I'm use to men spoiling. Who knows, a change could help me maybe even this time around I'll spoil the man. It's strange I'm thinking like this; Antonio bought me my first car. It was a brand new Porsche how beautiful it was! He bought me so many diamonds as well. There's nothing to good for me. Everything I asked for I got it. Lots of women would think I was insane to leave such a good thing. The only thing Antonio didn't give me was respect, respect, respect! He started treating me like I was nothing anymore. I was sick and tired of him talking to me any kind-ah way! I took all the bull-crap I could from him. My only problem was doing drugs. I was a drug addict with a capital A, but I still had high morals and values. I just made up my mind to leave his abusive behavior and I refused to accept anymore of Antonio's mess. I'll never go through that again."

Antonio's actions towards her were part of the reason she ended up at the center and she was very glad that she was trying to do something positive with her life.

"Oh my God if I had-nah left Antonio when I did I'd probably been caught up in that hit they put out on him. Thank you God, I wasn't caught in that hit. I wouldn't even be around now having these thoughts going through my mind. I have so much to tell my son or daughter who will soon be born into such a sinful world. I have a funny feeling something strange about this baby, but I just can't understand what it is at this time. Something is telling me to beware."

She felt unease about having such thoughts and feelings. She just couldn't help the thoughts and feelings she was experiencing. She even felt that it was natural to have such thoughts and feelings.

Her thoughts were suddenly interrupted by a knock on the door. "Who is it?" She said with a soft voice.

"It's your favorite doctor," Shawn said smiling.

"Come on in," she shouted.

As Shawn was entering the room, Gena noticed the purple package he was carrying under his arm as if he was trying to conceal it.

Gena smiled and asked, "what is that you have with you Shawn?"

"It's for you my love, here, open it and see."

As she began un-wrapping the gift she was amazed; a beautiful pair of pearl earrings.

"Their beautiful, but I can't accept them, they must-ah cost a fortune."

Shawn sneered saying, "don't worry about the cost. The most important thing is do you like them?"

"Of course I do, I love them would more of the words to say. They are so lovely."

"Not as lovely as lovely as you are Gena, there's nothing I've seen more beautiful than you."

As Gena continued smiling from the excitement, Shawn gazed into her eyes saying, "there is nothing in this world more beautiful than you Gena!"

Gena hugged him saying, "Shawn you sure have a way with words and a way of being affectionate as well as with your most unsuspecting, gorgeous gifts."

Shawn held her tighter saying, "you sure have a way of holding a man."

"I'm not holding any man I'm holding my man. I have no doubt that this day is the beginning of a wonderful relationship to come for you and I Shawn."

Shawn was caught by surprise from her words and said, "what can I say Gena?"

"Don't say anything just kiss me!" Their lips were glued together as if they were trying to set a record for the longest kiss ever. As they continued kissing, thoughts ran through Gena's mind. "Only if Shawn could read my mind; I feel so faint, but this isn't the right time or place."

After the kissing had finally come to a halt, Gena asked, "what are you thinking about Shawn?"

With a big smile on his face he answered, "just holding you in my arms I feel so faint, but I know this is not the right time or place."

"That's funny because I was just thinking the exact same thing, but even if this was the right time and place I still couldn't sleep with you because of the baby. I wouldn't want you to miscarriage or anything like that!"

"No we wouldn't want that," he said gently.

"Don't worry my love I clearly understand you!"

"I knew you would my handsome prince."

Shawn walked over to the window and gazed out at the hills calling Gena at the same time.

"Come over here and look at how lovely the snow on the hills looks."

Gena gazed out the window saying, "Oh gosh that is so beautiful!" She yelled and grabbed his hand.

Shawn smiled back saying, "in a few weeks you'll look out this window and see deer' lined up as if they're about to go to war. I have videos of the deer' standing on these hills and I would have to show them to you one day."

"Sure Shawn, I would love to see them one day!"

"Gena, it's getting late. Are you hungry?"

"Yes, I didn't realize how late it was. Their serving dinner would you like to join me for dinner?"

Shawn excitedly accepted the offer, "of course I would I'm starving."

As they entered the cafeteria Shawn spotted a friend of his named Mo and introduced him to Gena. The three of them sat together eating dinner discussing the weather.

Mo smiled asking, "so Gena, how long do you anticipate it will be before you have your baby?"

"Not soon enough," she said jokingly.

Mo laughed saying, "so… Do you have any intentions on becoming Misses Bomoski one day?"

Gena started laughing at the question not sure if he was joking or serious so she said, "why don't you ask Shawn that question!"

Before he could get the question out his mouth Shawn said," I sure hope so." They all began to laugh as if they were on some kind of laughing gas.

Everything seemed so funny to everyone until Gena face expression changed as she said, "ooooh, ooh!"

"What's wrong?" Shawn asked touching her shoulder.

"It's my stomach; it feels like the baby is trying to push his way out of my stomach. It's probably his way of letting me know he was hungry too."

Shawn said, "when you say he your saying you know it's a boy?"

"No, I don't know; I don't know what made me say he. Well I believe it's going to be a boy at least that's what I'm hoping for!"

Shawn said, "well I believe it's gonna be a boy."

Gena smiled saying, "I hope your right."

"Yeah, I do too. Maybe he'll grow up to be a doctor like me."

"Maybe!" Gena said rubbing her stomach.

Mo was about six feet tall, well-tanned complexion, 200 pounds, and had dark, dark eyes to go along with his dark black hair.

Just before completing their dinner, there was loud shouting coming from the hallway just outside of the cafeteria. As soon as Shawn and Mo heard the commotion they rushed to see what was going on!

It was one of the patient's shaking and trembling as if she had just seen a ghost.

When Gena got in the hallway to see what was going on, she recognized the young lady and approached her. She took hold of her hand asking, "what's bothering you?"

Mo said, "the girl name is Paula."

"What's bothering you Paula?" Gena softly asked, "what's the problem?" Paula answered, "she's in my room 12-b!"

"Who's in 12-b Paula? Who? Talk to me, who Paula?"

"It's Karen she's dead."

With a shocking face expression Gena said, "What? Oh my God!"

Shawn said to Mo, "let's go and see. Maybe we can revive her before it's too late. Quick, let's hurry!"

When they entered 12-b, they discovered that it was too late. Karen's eyes were wide open, her mouth filled with saliva, and her face cold as ice. There was no chance of reviving her!

As Mo took a closer look around the bed the body was laying on, he noticed something on the bed next to the body.

"It's a needle," Paula yelled out.

Gena shockingly said, "yeah it is a needle I believe she took an overdose!"

"So do I?" Shawn said surprisingly staring at the body.

Gena said, "would someone please cover her up?"

"Sure," Mo said grabbing the sheet on the floor next to the bed.

Shawn called the morgue; they arrived within an hour and took the body away. As Gena stood by watching she thought, "that could have been me if I hadn't decided to give up drugs." Gena then asked, "I wonder how she got drugs in here?"

"I don't know, but there will be an investigation starting first thing in the morning," Shawn said angrily.

"Ohhhh I wish this baby would stop turning flips in my stomach."

As they left Karen's room, Shawn said, "well he should be a very active child maybe a gymnastic," Shawn smiled.

"I'm amused of your confidence."

Shawn hugged her, trying to distract her from her discomfort saying, "I sure hope we be together Gena,"

"I'm sure we will," she said with a look of happiness as she said, "I still can't get over what happened to her today."

"Allow me to walk you to your room. I know you're tired of standing with that heavy load your carrying. Naturally I'm speaking of our bundle of joy."

"Yes, I'll do that and still I fall asleep, I'll be thinking of you Mr. Bomoski," she smiled gazing into his eyes.

"That's wonderful to know my sweet love so do know I'll be doing the same thing; thinking of you till I fall asleep."

"Goodnight my dear."

"Goodnight."

As Shawn began to walk away, Gena shouted out to him, "I had a very nice time today Shawn!"

"So did I!" He said throwing up his hands in the air.

As soon as Gena closed the door she went and sat on her bed and started thinking about Paula. Her emotions became very intense that she started to allow tears to flow down her face.

"Paula is so young and beautiful; Karen's death should open other patient's eyes around here. Then they'll see that their cheating themselves by still using drugs in the center. When will people learn that drugs ain't nothing but-ah killer? Oh thank God I'm no longer a user."

Gena started yarning, "it's been a long day; it's time for me to turn in."

Awakening the next morning, Gena laid there for a moment thinking and said softly reaching for the book on her nightstand, "I haven't read in a while; I got to catch up on my reading." The book was called *Crack Destruction*. "Only two more chapters," she said out loud.

As she continued to read she noticed how fast the time had gone by, and she then became curious as to what was on television. She began flicking from channel to channel, but didn't find anything of interest to watch. Then she heard the bell ringing, and that sound reminded her that lunch was being served. "Let me go and see what they are serving."

Gena entered the cafeteria and said to herself, "ummm, that looks good, baked chicken and corn."

Gena could hear a voice calling her from behind, and began to scan through the cafeteria to see who was calling her name and it was Paula. "Oh hi Paula," she said waving her hand.

"Come and join me," Paula said smiling. "Sure…" Gena said smiling back.

When Gena finally made it to the table, Paula asked, "how did you sleep last night?"

"I guess okay."

"Girl… I couldn't sleep-ah lick."

"Paula you must get your rest, it's important that you get enough sleep."

Paula was five-feet-two, 110 pounds, pretty cocoa butter skin, pearly white teeth, dark brown eyes, long black hair, and was built like a coca-cola bottle. She was in her early thirties.

"I know Gena, but I just couldn't get Karen off my mind at all last night."

"I know it's a shame isn't it?"

"She was so young!"

"Yes, she was very young, but we have to live on child so after you finish eating please go get you some rest Paula."

"I'll try," she said yarning.

Gena and Paula sat at the table talking a little while longer after they'd eaten lunch, than they both decided it was time to go.

As they began walking back to their room, they both were thinking the same thing; as long as they had been at the center, the two of them had never struck up a conversation with each until Karen's death occurred.

They decided to take a walk in the yard, and as they walked, Paula asked, "how's your relationship coming along with Shawn? And don't give me that ain't nothing going on jive. I see the way you two carry on when y'all together."

"Please…. Girl, he's so nice. I just hope he can put up with me and this load I'm carrying."

"Don't worry, I can look and see that he likes you a lot."

"Hope your right."

"Of course I'm right girl, I been here almost eight-months, and I ain't never seen Shawn take a patient the way he takes you. You're so lucky!"

"No, he's the lucky one," they laughed. "Let's sit down somewhere, I been on my feet to long, their killing me."

"I know how you feel girlfriend. I felt the same way when I was carrying my baby."

"You have a baby?" She asked surprisingly.

"Yepp, I sure do, he's three now."

"Where is he?"

"Parents have him."

"You must miss him so much!"

"I think about him every day, I wish I could see him!"

"I wish you could too," Gena put her hand around Paula's shoulder. "Don't worry, God will make a way for you."

"Gena you sure have a way of making me feel better. Thank you so much for caring about how I feel!"

"That's what friends are for, come on, let's go."

"Are you sure you can make it right now?"

"Of course I can, now come on girl, let's go."

As they headed back towards the center, Paula spotted an old friend of hers named Cookie. Cookie was tall and muscular, short brown hair, dark black eyes, around hundred-thirty –pounds.

Paula stopped walking and said, "I know that bitch."

"Who?"

"That sorry bitch standing over there. She and I had some problems awhile back when the streets were in my life. I sure hope she don't bring her sorry ass in my face. I can't stand her signifying, no good short mixed up ass!"

"You should forgive and forget."

"I know, but it's hard to forgive when you know someone that's in the same building with you, who one time had you set up for a rape!"

"Rape!" She said with rage.

"Yes rape. She told me she had something for me at her boyfriend's house; only thing waiting for me there was two of her boyfriend friends, and they acted like I owed them something. She introduced them to me and left me alone in the kitchen with them, saying she would be back in about ten minutes. I said cool, don't forget to bring back the beer, and she said, "what kind?" I said, "Coors," then she said, "don't worry I got you covered, see you shortly. As soon as she left, one of the guys reached over and put his hand on my thigh. I had on a short red mini skirt. I asked him not to do that. "Nannn, don't worry lil-lady we not goin hurt you." When he said my heart started pumping ninety miles a minute. One got up and stood behind me while I was sitting in the chair. He bent over me and started sliding his hand up and down my pussy. I asked him to stop, but he said, "shut up bitch." The other guy got on his knees in front of me and started pulling down my panties. I tried to jump up out the chair, but the one behind me grabbed me and slammed me on the kitchen floor, and there I was, lying on the floor getting screwed every way you could think of. I was crying like a baby; I felt like dying. I kept saying to myself over and over in my mind, this can't be happening to me, but it was, and that bitch helped set it up. I'll never forgive that hoe."

"I feel so sad for you." They both stood with tears running down their faces.

"The bad part about the whole thing is, my three-year-old son is by one of the rapists," she said with tears rapidly falling.

"God no....! You must feel terrible, I'm sorry for you Paula!"

"Don't, I just wish I could get back at that wormy bitch."

As they got closer to Cookie, cookie immediately recognized Paula, and with a look of shock on her face, Cookie said, "what's up?"

Before Cookie could say another word Paula started blazing her. "You're a dirty bitch! How can you look me in my face after what you had done to me?"

Suddenly a left fist came out of nowhere landing on Cookie's right eye. "I'll kill you, you no good bitch," Paula shouted out as she continued throwing more blows on Cookie's face.

Gena cried out, "please stop Paula, please you're gonna kill-er!"

Gena wanted to break them up, but she knew she wasn't physically ready because of the pregnancy, but others who stood around watching pulled Paula off of her.

When they were finally loose Cookie cried out, "I'm goin get you back bitch, your day coming bitch."

"Oh, I'm not through with you bitch! Now I know where your ass at, I'm goin make you pay for what happened to me tramp!"

"Paula, let's sit down and rest for a minute, my legs are killing me."

"All right, I know you're tired."

"Yes I am and you should be too."

"Not at all, I never felt better. Just knowing where she's at makes me feel good inside!"

"I wish you'd forget about her right now," she said sitting down.

"Okay," she said taking her seat.

"Girl… where did you learn to punch like that? You look like Liston back there, they both laughed.

"So tell me Paula, when are you planning on leaving this place?"

"Actually, I don't think I'm ready for the streets right now. Nope, not that I don't want too; I just think I'm not ready to leave this place yet. My mind is not quite clear yet. I still have thoughts and urges for drugs to damn often. I'm gonna stick around here till I'm sure I'm ready. I ain't in no hurry to get back out there in the streets."
"Whenever you do get out of here, I hope we can continue to be friends!"

"Why of course, don't be silly."

"I will always stay in touch with you no matter where I'm at."

"I believe you. Where will you be staying when you leave here?"

"Actually, I have no idea, but something will come up."

"I'm sure it will! Can I ask you a personal question?"

"Sure, go for it."

"What was your first experience with love-making like?" She smiled.

Gena smiled, "if I can think back that far in the past. Okay, I remember this handsome boy name Tee. Girl…he was so built, muscles everywhere. He was on the high school football team. Girl, everyday he would ask me if he could walk me home. Sure, I would say, but not to my front door, and everyday he would ask me the same old question. "Why can't I walk you to your door?" I would give him the same old answer; my parents don't take to blacks. He would just smile and say, "I understand." One day he was walking me home we spotted…"

Paula interrupted saying, "wait…a minute. You use to like black boys?" She smiled.

"Yes… I was in love with Tee. Now will you please let me finish telling you about my first relationship with a boy, geez. Okay, and one day Tee and I spotted this old abandoned car. When we got to the car we noticed that the seats let back."

Paula laughed, "not in the car girl."

"Girl shut up and let me finish please… So he let his seat back as far as it could go, and as he was lying back with his feet pressed against the dashboard, I spotted this big bulge poking out on the side of his pants. Being curious, I reached over and touched the bulge with my hand, and asked him what is that?" He said, "girl you know what that is."

"No I don't seriously. What is it, it feels so big?" He said, "it's my thang."

"I asked him could I see it. He unzipped is pants as he took it out. Girl… the biggest cock I ever saw in my life for a fourteen-year-old. I was so enthused. All I could think about was touching his hard long rod, so I reached over and gently took a grip of his black cucumber. Then I said wow, it feel so good. Then I slightly put my hair in a ponytail so it wouldn't get in the way if you know what I mean. Anyway, I started sucking that cock, and sucking that cock till I saw or should I say, felt something wet squirt inside my mouth, and I don't have to tell you what that was. You know I really didn't know what I was doing; the next thing I knew I was telling him to stick it in the pussy. Oh… girl, when he stuck his cock inside my hot pussy, felt like I was in heaven. I ain't never felt anything as good in my life that felt as good as that dick inside of my cunt. Seem like every day after school I was looking forward to Tee walking me home so he could make love to me over and over in that old beat up car. We had so much fun girl, but it all came to an end. Tee was found dead in the alley behind the school playground! I know for a fact he was murdered by somebody white all because he was fucking me. And believe me honey; I miss the hell out of that black beef. I think about him all the time!"

"Well since you liked black beef so much, why didn't you get you another black boy for some more black beef?"

"Girl is you kidding? I didn't want the same thing that happened to Tee' to happen to someone else so I decided after Tee came up dead I wouldn't get involved with another black boy! What about you Paula; what was your first time making out with a boy like?"

"Girl, I'll tell you about it later. Right now I'm about to go to my room and take me a cold shower, and look at a little television. Then I'm going to think about you and your first date with a boy and the way you two made love. Damn that sounded good to my ears."

"You're something else. I'll see you at dinner time."

"It depends on what they're serving. You take it easy."

"You too."

Gena made up her mind that she wasn't going to have the baby in no rehabilitation center.

Gena sat around reading most of the time, since the weather was pretty bad, and Christmas was only ten-days away.

As Gena lay still on the couch reading her novel, she began to say to herself, "no, it's getting late, I wonder what Paula doing?"

Suddenly someone knocked on the door, "come in, it's open. Why Shawn, what brings you this way?" She said smiling.

"Why you of course, I been thinking about you all day, and I have something I wanna ask you!"

"What's on your mind?"

"I think your special Gena, and I would like you to be my wife! Will you marry me Gena?!"

"Are you serious?!"

"Yes Gena, I love you, be mines forever!"

"Yes Shawn, I will marry you!"

"Great so what would you like; a church wedding or a house wedding?"

"Either one is fine with me," she said hugging his neck. "Hold it, I'd like a house wedding if that's okay with you!"

"That's fine with me, I'll let Mo know he's going to be my best-man, and I think our house will make the perfect place for the wedding."

"Owe....Shawn, this is the happiest day in my life, I love you!"

"I want you to be the happiest woman in the world Gena! I want you to check out of this place as soon as possible and I think first thing in the morning will be just the right time. That way you can spend the whole day getting use to your new home."

"Then tomorrow morning it shall be. I'll start packing the little stuff I do have tonight."

Shawn's face went from happy to sad. Shawn said, "there's something I got to know before you check out of here."

"I know that look Shawn, and if you're worried about whether or not I'm able to handle society again, don't be, I ain't never been more ready in my life. In fact, I'm more than ready. I'm about to be a mother soon, and a wife, and as long as I have you by my side I'll always be ready!"

"Good, you answered what was on my mind. Now, why don't we go and grab a cup of coffee together."

"Fine with me darling."

As they sat at the cafeteria table gazing into each other's eyes, Shawn said, "am I dreaming and if I am please don't wake me."

"No you're not dreaming, I'm over here sweetheart, and your over there. The words you hearing are also real. I love you Mr. Bomoski!"

Shawn smiled, "I love you too Misses Gena Bomoski!"

"O Shawn, I'm so excited!"

"So am I, I want our love to last a lifetime!"

"And so do I, but I heard those words before!"

"You may have, but you ain't never heard them come out of my mouth before. Now am I correct?"

"Yes Shawn, you're correct. O'boy, I almost forgot about Paula. I got-ah let-er know I'm leaving tomorrow. That's funny, I haven't seen her at all today, and that's unusual!"

Shawn put the coffee cup down saying, "maybe she's sleep or in the game room. You know how she likes video games."

Gena fumbled with her hair, "I don't think so she would-ah ask me to go with her. Something's wrong Shawn, I can feel it! I'm going to look for her!"

Shawn downed the rest of his coffee. "I'll help you, you check the game room, and I'll check her room."

Shawn and Gena checked everywhere they possibly could, but no sign of Paula.

Shawn spotted Gena and called out to her saying, "did you have any luck on the north wing?"

Gena gasped for breath. "No, no luck on that side, but there is one place I haven't checked."

Shawn's pager went off. "I have to get to a phone."

Gena kissed him. "You go and answer your pager, I'll find'er."

While Shawn headed to a phone, Gena continued looking for Paula and said to herself out loud, "now where in the world could this girl be? O'well, I guess I'll check my last destination, the washroom, and if she ain't there I give up."

Gena entered the washroom, "boy it's quiet as a church mouse in here, but I can feel it in my soul that I'm not the only one in this room. Someone is in here besides me."

Gena started looking sharply around the washroom, and then slowly started walking where she spotted the large green desk. As she approached the desk, she nervously bent over to see what was behind the desk. Bingo, there she was, in a kneeling position on the floor.

Gena cried out, "Paula, what is wrong with you?! Tell me what on God's Earth is wrong with you!"

Paula was in a state-of-shock, shaking and trembling like she's saw a ghost. Gena reached down to help her to her feet. "Are you okay Paula? Please... talk to me. Tell me what's wrong. I wanna help you; I'm your friend Paula!"

Paula just stood there looking into Gena's eyes speechless. Suddenly, Gena spotted the tiny white seal on the floor next to where she had helped Paula up.

Gena picked the white seal up and angrily said, "its dope in this seal, this is dope! Who did you get this stuff from? Who gave you this?"

Paula put her arms around Gena and started crying. Her words were hysterical as she spoke, "I don't wanna get nobody in trouble; I don't wanna get nobody in trouble."

Gena caressed Paula's hair, "just tell me who gave this shit to you?"

Paula hesitated with her words and cried out even more. "It was Mo! I'm sorry Gena! Please, you can't tell nobody, I don't want'em to lose his job. Promise me you want tell nobody."

Gena was shocked to learn that Mo was supplying drugs to the center to patients. She held Paula tighter, "this drug-dealing has to stop Paula! Mo's probably the one responsible for Karen's death!"

"Please, you can't tell on'em! Please!"

Gena let out a sigh. "When will you learn Paula, you are in here to get away from getting stoned and get it out of your mind. Look at-cha, you look-ah mess. Come on, let's go to my room so I can clean you up."

As they started walking, Paula said, "I'm sorry I hurt you. I promise it want happen again!"

When they got in Gena's room, she placed both locks on the door. Normally, she wouldn't bother to lock either one, but she didn't want Shawn to walk in on them and find Paula looking like she was strung out.

Gena turned the shower on while Paula slowly took her clothing off. As Gena turned to tell Paula the water was ready, she was hesitant to sneak as she watched Paula slip out of her candy apple red panties.

"The water is nice and warm girl, it should make you feel better," Gena said to herself as she watched Paula get into the tub. "She's a very nicely built woman. I ain't seen jet black hair on a woman's pussy before. Damn she has a nice round ass and nice chest. She looks like she never shot dope before in her life."

"Paula you have a nice built girl."

Paula couldn't understand a word Gena was saying because of the noise coming from the shower. "You have to speak up, I can barely hear you."

Gena loudly said, "I said you have a nice body, but you gonna lose it if you keep on messing with that shit."

Paula cut the water off and stepped out the tub saying. "look, I already told you I am sorry, and I promised you it wouldn't happen again. Now what more can I say to make you shut-up the drug talk? And besides, what made you come looking for me in the first place. After all, I'm still a grown woman."

Gena stared at Paula with the thought, "what a lovely figure."

"I was looking for you to let you know me and Shawn decided to get married, and to let you know I was leaving in the morning. I want you to be my maid of honor."

Paula was very excited, "o' Gena I'm so happy for you. Have y'all set a date?"

"No, not yet, but believe me honey, when we do you'll be the first to know. How does Christmas day sound to you?"

"It sounds good to me girl," she said with joy in her voice.

"Great."

"My girl is getting married."

"Yepp, and Christmas Day it shall be. I'll let Shawn know, I hope he agree with that day."

Paula looked into Gena's eyes with tears falling from hers. "I'm sorry about what happened today. You are truly a true friend!"

Tears ran down Gena's face, "let's forget it ever happened. I care about you Paula, and don't you ever forget that! Girl, this is going to be one of the best Christmases I ever had in my life, and you are going to be a part of it!"

Paula smiled, "thank you, you're such a nice person, and I'm glad I got the chance to meet you."

Gena smiled, "I'm glad I got the chance to meet you too."

Paula yarned, "give me a robe or something to put on, and by the way where is Shawn?"

"O' he got a beep on his pager and went to take care of it, but he's around here somewhere. He'll probably come knocking on my door any minute now."

"You are so lucky Gena to have a man like Shawn in your life. He's a very nice man."

Gena smiled, "I know and someday Mr. Right will be stepping into your life."

Paula put her hands over her mouth, "I hope you're right girlfriend."

"Of course I'm right, you're a very, very attractive lady, and a man would have to be double-blind not to want you, and from what I've seen, you have a wonderful figure. I wish I had the curves you got girl, you could pose for Playboy Magazine."

Paula laughed. "You really think I have the body of a model?"

"Yeah.... Girl, you have all that it takes. You have all the qualifications it takes to be one, and I know if I was a man I wouldn't think twice about looking at you if I saw you in a Playboy Magazine."

Paula walked away, "yeah right, I'll keep that in mind."

Gena kicked off her shoes deciding that she needed a shower too, and as she walked to the bathroom she thought, "I hope Paula take what I said serious and leave those damn drugs alone. She's very attractive; what I wouldn't give to have a body like hers. She's the first black woman I ever seen naked face to face. I pray to God she leaves those drugs alone, I don't want her to stay in this place forever. She need to be out there with her son; he almost three-years-old, and she haven't spent two whole days with him. It's a shame for any mom not to spend any time with their child. In fact it's a disgrace. I can understand Paula's situation; she's trying to recover. She don't know this place can't really help her; she can get all the counseling in the world, but she gonna have to be the one to say in her mind "no to drugs" nobody else can do it for'er. I can pray for her every day of the week, but she gonna have to help herself, and only she knows what she want! I'm going through the same thing she's going through, and I had to make up my own mind. In God's eyes I'm no better than she is, but I know I had to take the first step in order for God to take the second step. Sometimes even my mind drifts back to the time I was using so the urge would reappear. I just use my God to fight off the temptation. I just pray the same prayer each time; I say "Lord, please don't let these drugs enter into my life again, and God keeps me away from the drugs; and drugs away from me."

Paula opened the bathroom door and shouted out, "I'm gone, I'll see you later on."

Gena stuck her head out the shower, "okay.... See you later."

Soon after Paula left, Gena could hear a knock on the door, and yelled out, "I'm coming," she said slipping into her bathrobe. "I wonder who that could be."

"Who is it?" she called out.

"It's Mo, I need to speak with you."

Gena put her hands in the air, letting out a sigh. "What's he doing here? I don't want to see him especially after what he did to Paula." Gena opened the door. "Hi Mo, what brings you this way?"

Mo smiled, "hey Gena, I heard the good news, and I wanted to be the first to congratulate you, and…. being that I'm gonna be the best man, I want to do something special for you guys. I came by to ask you if you were interested in getting your wedding gown custom-made since I know this tailor who specializes in making wedding clothes."

Gena smiled, "why Mo, it's a lovely idea, have you talked to Shawn about it?"

Mo patted his hands smiling, "yes I talked to Shawn and he sent me to ask you so here I am."

Mo shook Gena's hand, "good I'll contact Mrs. Ross first thing is the morning, that way she can go to your new home and size you up. Well, I'll be going now, you have a nice day."

Gena nodded her head, "you too Mo, good-bye."

Gena closed the door, "Mo really not a bad person; he just got to stop giving these patients here drugs to use. Ooh wee," she said as her face expression turned into pain. "Boy you gonna have to stop kicking mommy like a football. I know you ready to come in the world; hold your horses. It won't be long, just a few more weeks. Then you'll be able to kick all you want." Another kick came from the baby. "Oohh," she cried. "Thanks for kicking me; you just reminded mommy that she has a check up this week. I almost forgot, thank you very much. Now you don't have to kick mommy anymore." Another kick came, as to say, you're welcome mom. "I see we have a great understanding already, and you ain't even in the world yet. This is gonna be wonderful," Gena smiled.

Gena sat on the bed still talking to herself, "Lord! I believe I'm marrying a man who truly does care about me. No matter what my previous life was like he still wanna be with me. He know I'm an ex dope user; not to mention I'm pregnant too with another man's child. That's why I love'em so much! O' thank you god so much for bringing a man like Shawn in my life. I can't wait to get out this place so I can start my life all over. This time I wanna find me a job. Maybe set-up some type of program to help people who are on drugs. I truly don't wanna sit around the house collecting dust in my hair. I wanna be a part of something positive; something I can feel proud about so God can look down on me and say, "job well done Gena." I know I'm use to having everything my way, but not anymore. I wanna be the one giving this time instead of getting all the time. I don't need the fast life anymore; I know where it leads too. I'll be so damn glad when I have this baby so Shawn and I can have sex. I miss sex so much; it's been almost nine months now. O'well that's the way love goes. I'll just keep doing what I been doing; taking these cold showers. I guess I'll turn on the radio, ooh, that's my jam.

Gena stood up and danced to the music pretending she had a partner. "*The Temptations* are definitely a hit," she excitedly said, "I got to hurry up and have this baby so I can dance like I want too, and go to me a concert. I wouldn't mind seeing *The Temptations* live; these guys can sing. As a matter of fact I saw in the newspaper the other day they suppose to be at Cobo Arena next month. I might be able to catch that concert."

Gena glanced at the clock on her dresser. "It's getting close to supper, I wonder where Shawn could be. He normally would'ah checked on me by now. I guess he's busy with his work right now."

Someone knocked on the door, "come in."

Shawn came in smiling, "close your eyes, I have something for you." Gena closed her eyes. "Now you may open them."

Gena opened her eyes and stared at the engagement ring Shawn held in his hand. "Do you like it?" He asked sliding the ring on her finger.

Gena hugged him, "like it, I love it, it's beautiful!"

"I'm glad you like it, I had it custom-made just for my beautiful bride."

Gena put the ring up close to her eyes. "Shawn, how did you know my ring size? My finger ain't that readable."

Shawn laughed, "well it's like this, I was married once before, and you and my late wife look so much alike, and you remind me so much of her. You both look to be about the same size, and I figured you both had the same size hands. I see I was right."

"Oh Shawn," she held him tightly.

"You see Gena, earlier when my pager went off, it was for me to come down and pick up the ring."

Gena slowly pushed away. "You devil you, I want to know one thing if it's not too personal."

"You don't have to say another word. You wanna know how did my wife die?"

"Why I see you're also a mind-reader. So tell me, how did she die?"

Shawn's face turned from joy to sadness. "Well, one day I was here working late and I heard my name being called over and over on the loud speakers. I could sense something was wrong; so when I finally got to the front desk the secretary looked like she was about to cry. I knew than for sure something was wrong. I said, "what's wrong Kathy? She said, "it's your wife Mr. Bomoski. She's on her way to Receiving Hospital!"

"For what?" I asked. "She said she didn't know, but she did know. Finally she broke down, tears running down her face. She said, "someone said she took an overdose, I'm not sure!"

"I rushed down to the hospital thinking to myself; she got to be in the emergency room. I was looking like a wreck that night." Gena grabbed his hand, tears falling from her eyes. "When I got to her, the doctor walked up to me and said, "sorry sir, she didn't pull through."

"I asked him how did she die, and he said it was from an overdose of cocaine. He said her brain had slipped into a coma, but the drugs are what caused her death! I just grabbed me a seat next to her body. I still couldn't believe what had happened. I didn't even know she had a drug problem. I kept saying to myself over and over again, how could this be? Still to this day, I still wonder how she got hold to drugs. Who did she know that used drugs? I couldn't think of a soul. I mean we never went anywhere where drugs were involved, and we only had two or three friends that came over to the house, and none of them did drugs. Not that I could possibly know of! The only friend she had coming over often was Tina, and Tina didn't drink or smoke; she's a health fanatic. The only friends I have over to the house are Crag and Mo, and they don't do drugs either."

Gena thought to herself, "Mo say not to do drugs, but he damn sure sell them. He's probably the one slipping dope to your wife. It's a strong possibility; I wouldn't put it pass him. I damn sure wouldn't trust'em! He's capable of trying to get me to do drugs again especially after what he did to Paula. That slick, slimy bastard!"

"You see Gena, you remind me of her so much. By the way her name was Linda. You two could pass for sisters. It's like a dream come true to find another woman who looks so much like her. And that's why I want you to be my wife. She meant everything to me. I would have given her the world to get her back. I guess God has his time set for everyone to die. Her time was up, I have you now, and I promise I will do everything in my power to keep you happy. I love you Gena!"

Gena rubbed his face. "I love you too Shawn and I can't wait to be Mrs. Bomoski," she smiled.

Shawn pulled her hand away from his face. "Tomorrow is gonna be a busy day for you; you better get some rest. I'll see you in the morning."

Gena grabbed his hands. "Don't leave right now. Can't you stay a little longer?"

"I would love too, but I do have a job to do like other patients to see."

"Of course you do, but do drop back by," she said smiling.

Shawn opened the door. "I will honey. Maybe we can have dinner together. I hear their serving steaks."

"Oooo, that sounds good. I'll see you at dinner."

"Good-day," Shawn darted out the door.

Gena's mind drifted back to Paula. "I wonder what Paula doing?" A knock came on the door. "It's open."

"Girl, I was just thinking about you, how you feeling!"

Paula lifted her hands. "Girl I feel terrific thanks to you. After that talk we had earlier, I know I'm not gonna mess up no more."

"I pray that you don't!"

"I give you my word Gena! No and no, better than that. I swear on my own life I want get caught up in that mix again!"

"Speaking of your son, what's his name?"

"His name is Stan; he's very handsome from what I could see on his pictures my mother sent me. Girl... he has some of the prettiest eyes; they hazel brown. I now the little girls gonna drive him crazy. He's definitely going to break some woman's heart one day."

"They both laughed, "I can imagine."

"He's definitely gonna break some woman's daughter heart with those color eyes alone. A woman would fall madly in love with his eyes alone."

Paula bows her head? "I just want him to have everything I didn't have in life. I want'em to know his mother!"

Gena put her hand on Paula's shoulder. "Of course he will know you. Don't worry yourself over nothing. You just get yourself together in here, and I guarantee you' you two will be together in no time."

Paula wiped her tears. "Yeah, I guess you're right. I know my mother is spoiling him to death."

"Where did you say your mother live?"

"Actually I lied about my son living thousands of miles away. I was ashamed to tell you the truth. I didn't want you to know my child is right here in Michigan and I don't even know'em. My mother don't want anything to do with me at all. At least not till I get my life together. That's why I told you they lived many miles away. Actually my mother lives in southwest Detroit. She's lived there all of her adult life. She's originally from Pittsburgh. She moved to Detroit right after my father got out of high school. My father came up here first to find a job, and after he found work here they got married and bought a house on Bassett Street. They seemed happy together, but my mother explained to me how they decided to separate. She said they were having problems that I was too young to understand. I haven't seen my father since then. I don't know if he's living or dead. I even tried calling where he use to work only to find out that he didn't work there anymore. As I got older I start doing things on my own. My mother couldn't control me. First I started hanging out with my girlfriends all night partying. Then I started using all types of drugs to get high on. First I smoked weed, then I went from weed to popping pills, and from popping pills to doing cocaine. I turned tricks day and night to supply my high. A lot of times I would ask myself what are doing to yourself Paula. I could never come up with an answer. It's sad to say, but I even turned tricks under my mother's roof. I just couldn't control myself. My mother would come home and find me lying naked in my bed stoned out of my mind. I couldn't even explain to her why I was like that! I knew I had a serious problem. I thought I could control it, but I couldn't. As time moved on I ended up in a situation no woman never wants to experience. I was raped!" She started crying.

Gena wiped the tears from Paula's eyes and hugged her. "Everything is gonna be okay now, you're gonna be fine, I promise!"

Paula put her hand on Gena's shoulder, with tears running. "I have to get out of here so I can get my son and raise him like a mother suppose too. I know I can be a good mother."

"Yes you can, and I'll do all I can to help you, you're my best-friend. I want you to raise your soul. O' my God, look at the time, we been talking so long girl. Dinner done creep up on us, let's go eat girl. They're serving steaks too."

Gena opened the door to find Shawn standing there getting ready to knock. Shawn smiled saying, "I was just coming to get you. O' you have company, hi Paula."

"Hi Shawn, how are you?" She smiled.

"Fine, thank you. What's wrong, you look like you've been crying!"

"It's nothing to worry about, now let's go out, I'm starving."

After dinner Shawn said, "they are showing a pretty good western movie in the dayroom. Why don't we all go check it out?"

Paula wiped her mouth with her napkin and said, "sounds good to me. I love western movies."

Gena slowly got out the chair saying, "o'ooo grabbing her stomach."

"What is it, are you okay? Shawn asked putting his arm around her.

"It's just the baby again. Every time I eat something he has to let me know he enjoyed it too," they all laughed.

During the movie Shawn and Gena kept whispering back and forth to each. "I love you Shawn."

"I love you Gena." Finally Paula had enough and yelled out. "Will you two shut the hell up…? I ain't never in my entire life in that damn much love. Now shut the hell up and enjoy the movie please…!"

Gena said, "girl one day you'll be getting married and doing the same thing we're doing."

Paula laughed, "yeah right, that'll be the day; me get married, no I don't think so, no way."

"Why not?" Gena asked.

"Girl I like my freedom to much. I like to do what I want to do, and there's one more thing."

Gena smiled saying, "and what's that?"

Paula whispered, "I can't cook," they both laughed.

Shawn joined in saying, "cooking ain't everything Paula."

Still laughing Paula said, "I can't even scramble eggs."

Gena laughed. "Girl I wouldn't tell nobody else that if I was you."

"It's not funny Gena."

Gena was trying hard not to laugh. "I know girl, but I just can't help. I'm sorry, whew."

"Don't be girl I know you were only kidding with me. Well the movie is over. I guess I'll see you two in the morning."

At the same time they both say, "see you Paula."

Shawn smiled saying, "I think Paula's a nice girl!"

"Yes she is! You know Shawn I remember telling myself I was never getting worried again. Look at me now, getting ready to be your wife. I'll never say never again. I think we make a great couple, don't you?"

"Yes Gena, we do, and by the way did Mo talk to you today about getting our wedding clothes custom made?"

She cleared her throat. "Yepp he sure did. I told him it was fine with me as long as you agreed to it."

"I can't wait to set my eyes on you in that beautiful wedding gown. You're going to make me the happiest man in the world!"

Gena looked into Shawn's eyes with compassion. "I hope so Shawn. You already made me the happiest woman in the world when you proposed to me. I will be so glad when I drop this load I'm carrying so you can drop your load in me, if you know what I mean."

"I believe I do, and I can't wait either. Lord knows I can't wait."

When they got to Gena's door, Shawn placed his hand on the wall and leaned over and kissed Gena. Gena moaned, "ooo, ahh, o'Shawn you're a good kisser."

"And so are you. Your lips are soft as cotton, and sweet like honey."

Gena smiled, "it gets sweeter than this my love."

Shawn smiled, "I can imagine; I must go now. I have some work I must catch up on you get some rest. Goodnight sweetie."

After Shawn left, Gena sat on the bed watching television, talking to herself. "Tomorrow gonna be a big day for me. I'm finally leaving this place. I'm gonna miss being here. O'well life goes on. I hope everybody in here leaves. This ain't the place to be for no one. I remember when Frank was murdered; seems like every man I get something bad happen to'em. I sure hope nothing happens to Shawn. I pray to God nothing happens to him. Please Lord let our relationship last a lifetime. Poor Antonio, look at you. Who's the bitch now? O…Antonio all you did was argue, argue, argue. You stupid bitch this, no good bitch that, you can't even have fucking kids, your fuck'n wound no good. Yes Antonio, it hurt me to think I couldn't have kids. You were wrong about me. Gena started crying. I can have children, and I'm going to have your baby Antonio, your baby, and I'm a have many more, you'll see. If only you were still alive Antonio!" Gena laid back on her back and fell asleep falling into a deep dream.

"Please don't take my baby from me! Please don't take my baby, please don't take my baby!" She jumped up out her sleep looking around. "Man what a dream; some strangers from another planet was trying to take my baby from me. The more I cried out to the creature not to take my baby away, the further he got out of my sight. Boy I'm glad it was just a dream. Scared me; the mess out of me."

Gena could hear the birds singing outside her window. "Day break finally. Thank you God for another beautiful day! Let me get my lazy behind up. Shawn will be here soon. I hope Paula come by to say goodbye. What am I saying, she's my best friend. Of course she'll be by to see me off."

After washing up, Gena turned the television on hoping to catch the morning news before Shawn got there. She glanced at the clock on the dresser. "Damn, it's almost nine o'clock. I'm packed and ready to go." A knock came on the door. "I know that knock, "come in Paula."

Paula walked in with a big smile on her face. "Well hello to you too."

Gena walked up to her and hugged her around the back. "I knew it was you at the door. I knew you would be here to see your best friend off."

Tears were falling from Paula's eyes. "Are you kidding, I wouldn't miss this moment for nothing in the world! I'm gonna miss you Gena!"

Tears were running from Gena's eyes. "I'm gonna miss you too Paula! Now stop crying you're making me cry. We'll still see each other. I'll stay in touch even if I have to write you every single day!"

"I thought I would never be saying this, but I want you to know, I love you Gena so I'm gonna miss the hell out of you!"

"O' Paula, I love you too, don't you worry. I'll come visit you so much you'll think I never left."

While the two of them stood embraced, Shawn walked in. "Hello ladies. Man… the roads are so bad out today. I would'ah been here, but traffic is jammed up on the freeway especially on I-96; talk about slippery."

Gena walked over to the window. "Boy it is bad out. I was just wondering what was taking you so long to get here today. I just said to myself a minute ago, he should'ah been here by now."

"Well sweetheart as you can see, it's not my fault. So how are you this morning? I see you came to see your girl off. I know you two goin miss each other."

Paula smiled, "Yeah… I'm goin miss my girl, but I'm happy for'er. She truly deserve better than this place here."

Shawn smiled, "Yes she does. O'well Gena, you better check out. I'll put your luggage in the car."

Paula and Gena went to the front desk to get copies of Gena's release papers while Shawn loaded up the truck of his car with luggage."

After getting the release papers signed, Gena and Paula went to the car where Shawn was patiently waiting for them.

Tears start running down Paula's face. "Well Gena, I guess this is goodbye!"

Gena embraced her. "For now it is. You take care of yourself you hear, and please Paula, don't get involved with Mo and his bullshit okay!"

"Don't worry, I promise you I won't. I'm through with doing that shit!"

Gena kissed Paula on the lips. "I'm glad to hear you say that to me. Take care; I'll be in touch so please Paula don't forget you're in my wedding. I got to go now, I love you!" They hugged.

Paula stood waving goodbye as she watched the station-wagon drive away. The further the car got, the more the tears fell from her eyes.

Gena looked back, "I'm really gonna miss her!"

"I know you are sweetheart, but you two will be back together again before you know it."

"Yeah… I guess you're right. It sure is slippery out here today."

Shawn entered the highway. "Yes it is. Now you see why it took me so long to get to you. The salt trucks haven't even came out yet, and it's been snowing every since six this morning."

Gena stared at the snow on the highway. "I see they haven't. It's cold out; even if the salt trucks do come, I don't think it'll do any good."

Out of the blue the car started skidding and became uncontrollable. Shawn was doing everything he could to gain control of the car, but the more he turned the steering wheel, the worse the sliding became on the icy road. Suddenly the car started gliding towards the side of the road where other cars were already wrecked and stranded.

Shawn cried out, "Lord I hope I don't slide into nobody!"

Gena could see that that's just what was going to happen as she cried out. "O'God please don't let this happen to us, please God! I come too far to lose my baby, please Lord!"

The car crashed right smack into the side door of a 1951 Ford. Boom was the last sound Gena heard as the impact knocked her unconscious.

It took the ambulance forty-five minutes to get to them. Shawn was okay and was trying everything he could to revive Gena.

After fighting their way through the jammed traffic, the ambulance had finally made it to where Shawn stood signaling for them with his hands waving in the air. "Over here!" He yelled out.

Hours later Gena had finally came out of her blackout, and her first thoughts were of her baby as she looked down and at her now empty stomach. Tears started rolling down her face as she said, "O' my God, my baby. God no, not my baby, why Lord? Please tell me why…?"

The doctor, nurses, and Shawn entered the room. Shawn was the first to speak.

"O' thank God, you finally come too. Why are you crying? Everything is okay!"

Gena put her hands over her eyes. "What about my baby?"

Shawn smiled, "the baby is fine."

Gena's face expression turned into joy. "O' thank God! What a miracle!"

Shawn took her by the hands. "The doctor wanna run some tests on him."

Gena excitedly threw her hands in the air. "I knew it was gonna be a boy, I knew it!"

"Have you thought of a name for him?"

"Yes, as a matter of fact I have. I'm gonna name him Antonio."

The doctor interrupted. "I'm sorry I got to disturb you two. How are you feeling Mrs. Bomoski?"

"I'm fine Doc, how's my baby doing?"

"I ran some tests on him; every one of them is excellent. There's one thing distinguished under his right eye, and I can't quite make it out what it could be. Let me put it to you like this, his birthmark is in an unusual place."

"I hope it's not that bad."

"You see Mrs. Montero, it's something like a scar, and it's right up under his eye."

Gena started saying, "it's amazing how the Lord works!"

The doctor smiled. "Do you know something I don't know Mrs. Montero?"

"Yes Doc, I can explain it to you. You see my late husband had a scar under his right eye, and everyone called him Scarface. Now my son has the same mark on his face. That's just God's way of letting me know my late husband has heard my voice. Isn't that something?"

Doc said, "it's strange, but amazing also I would say."

Gena laughed, "the funniest thing is I haven't even seen the baby yet and I already know who he looks like."

Doc smiled, "well Mrs. Montero I can fix that. Why don't we take you to see'em right now?"

Shawn said, "are you sure you're up to moving right now sweetheart? If not we can maybe arrange for the baby to be here, couldn't we Doc?"

"Sure we can. I'll have one of my nurses bring him down right away."

Gena smiled, "o' thank you Doc."

Fifteen minutes later the nurse arrived with the five-pound, eight-ounce baby boy.

The nurse smiled, "hey Mrs. Montero guess who? He's a little doll, here's your mommy."

Gena smiled as the nurse handed her the baby. "O' he's so cute just like I pictured him. This is Antonio all over, scar and all. I can't believe it; I know for sure there's a God, and he has answered my prayers. I'll never forget December 16th for as long as I live!"

December 19, 1962

Three days later, doctor and nurses entered Gena's room. Well Gena, I come today with good news. I see no reason to keep you and the baby here any longer so if you like too, you can leave today."

"That's wonderful Doc, I'll call Shawn and let him know the good news. I know he can't wait to get me home. I only been here a few days and already he has bought me what looks like the flower shop and every sympathy card in Michigan."

Doc laughed, "I can see he truly loves you!"

Gena checked out the hospital, and during their drive home, Shawn said with his eyes glued to the road checking for icy spots, "I hope you like your new home. I'm gonna do all I can to make you and the baby happy. I been thinking; we gonna have to put the wedding off until you're healthy enough to mingle. I say shoot three months from now should be okay. What you think?"

"I agree three months is fine with me. I love you so much Shawn. I don't want nothing to ever come between us. I need you in more ways than one!"

"I need you too Gena. Well, you're almost there. See the sign over to your left that reads (Welcome to Bloomfield Township, the home of Ranch Style Homes.")

Gena couldn't believe her eyes as she watched Shawn pull into the driveway. "These homes are gorgeous."

"Well Gena this is it."

"I like it already, and I haven't even seen the inside yet."

"It's even more beautiful to the summer time."

"I can imagine," she smiled.

"I hope you like the inside as well as you like the outside."

"I'm sure I will."

Gena walked inside holding the baby smiling. "Oooh it's lovely in here. You could'nah decorated this living room."

Shawn smiled, "of course I did."

Gena spotted a painting of herself hanging on the wall. "No, it can't be? How did you get a picture of me to have painted like that? It's so lovely."

"I took your I.D. from the front office back at the center, and I took it to a good friend of mine who just happens to be a painter. He's the best in his profession."

"I see he is; it must'ah cost a fortune."

"No my dear, actually it didn't cost me anything. My friend and I go back a long way so he did this painting for me on the strength of."

Gena smirked, "you have a talented friend."

"Yeah very talented. Come let me show you the rest of the house."

After Shawn finished giving her a tour of the house, Gena sighed. "Boyy this is a big house. I love it and I'm beat honey. If you don't mind I'm gonna watch me a little television."

"Of course I don't mind. By the way do you remember the story I told you about the deer? Would you like to see that video?"

"I would love too."

Shawn put the tape on and narrated as Gena watched.

After the tape went off, Gena glanced over and saw that the baby was still sound asleep. Shawn said, "now my love I have one more room to show you," he smiled.

"I thought I saw all the rooms."

"You have, all but this one. This one here is sort of a surprise. Grab the baby and let's go see the surprise."

"O' he still sleep, let'em sleep."

When Shawn opened the door to the surprise room, Gena's eyes lit up. "Oh my God, Shawn this is too much. You got'em everything."

"Yes my love and I want to give'em more. When we are married he'll be like my very own son that I never had. He's a part of me now."

Gena hugged him. "Ohhh Shawn, you are so good to me. I'm so lucky to have you in my life."

"No Gena, I'm lucky to have you. I guess you can say we're lucky to have each other. Ohhh Gena darling, I have so much I wanna share with you!"

"And I have something I wanna share with you too, and I can't wait for that day to come."

Shawn smiled, "neither can I. Did you hear something?"

"Yes I did; it must be the baby, he's probably up now. Let's go see what's the problem with him. He's probably hungry again, little joke can eat."

When they got back downstairs the baby was woke. Gena picked him up. "What's the matter with mommy little pootsie-wootsie? Mommy right here. Oooh, I see you made a stank-stank."

Gena changed the diaper while Shawn searched for a channel to watch on television.

"We're expecting two more inches of snow by midnight. I'll be so damn glad when summer gets here."

Shawn turned around noticing Gena breast-feeding the baby, and thought to himself. "What'ah sweet looking breast and it's another that matches tucked away. I'll be glad when it's my turn to suck on them pretty nipples."

Gena spotted him staring. "And just what are you thinking about?"

Shawn was smiling. "Do you really wanna know?"

"Yes I really wanna know, now tell me."

"I was just thinking if only I was Antonio right now. It must be nice; he ain't stop smacking yet," he laughed.

Gena laughed. "Come on over here my boy." Shawn wanted his turn. "I want you to take the other breast and suck till you get enough milk." She pulled her other breast out. "Come on now, it ain't goin bite-cha."

Shawn started sucking and Gena quickly laid the baby down. "Ohhh Shawn, ooh that feel good. I ain't had this feeling in so…long. I wish I could sleep with you, but I have something just as good baby. I'm goin give you the biggest surprise of your life."

A surprise it was. Shawn could feel Gena's hand unzipping his pants, and she slowly reached in the slot of his boxer shorts pulling out his semi-hard cock through the opening. She began massaging his now brick hard cucumber with her soft cotton lips. Using her hands to keep her hair from interfering with her stroke as she pulled her mouth away saying, "how does it feel, you like this?"

Shawn closed his eyes. "Ooh Gena don't stop. Damn that feels good."

Gena rubbed harder up and down his cock saying, "cum baby, cum in my mouth, cum baby."

"Ahhh," he sighed as he came. "I love you Gena. I know once you fully recover we goin have big fun together."

"Yes we are." Placing her tongue in his mouth, kissing him continuously, Gena pulled away saying, "oh Shawn, Christmas is right around the corner, and I don't have any money to get you anything."

"Gena darling, don't worry about it. I'm goin give you some money, say like a couple thousand dollars so you can do whatever you wish with it."

"O' Shawn you're too much."

"I love you Gena; I'll give you the world and all that's in it if you'll let me."

Gena hugged him. "You sure do have a way with words."

"Well how do these words sound?
"I…love…you…!"

Gena just smiled. "I love you too. By the way do you like spinach?

"Yes I most certainly do."

"Good because that is what we're having for dinner."

"Whatever you cook is all right with me," he said smiling.

"Good than spinach it shall be, and if you eat all your spinach, I'll be here to give you something sweet for dessert, if you know what I mean."

Shawn smiled, "what we waiting for? Let's get them pots to cooking."

Three months later March 30th...

Gena and Shawn decided they were going to get married April 1st.

Gena sat around the house talking to the baby most of the day while Shawn went off too work.

"Hey little-man, what's mommy bad baby doing? Well mommy sent out all the invitations. Now mommy just hope it don't rain on her wedding day, don't you? After all lil-man, there are such things as April showers. I just don't want the people we invited to have no...excuses. I can hear them now; the road was slippery, it was lightening so bad, just any old excuse not to come. We only have two more days before your mommy becomes Mrs. Bomoski. Wouldn't you like that?"

The baby smirked a smile as he listened. The telephone began to ring.

"Hi honey I know it's you."

Shawn was upset. "Hi sweetheart I called to you I can't believe what happened here today!"

"What's wrong now?"

"It's another one of my patients. We found another girl dead as a door knob, and she died from the same shit that killed Karen White. Why is this still happening? How in the hell are those drugs getting in here? Look baby, I'll be a little late getting home. Something wrong is going on in here and I'm goin get to the bottom of it to, see you later!"

Gena hung up. "Something is wrong, and it's Mo. Sooner or later I'm goin have to tell Shawn about him. I know I promised Paula I wouldn't say anything, but this killing can't keep going on like this. He can't keep giving them patients that shit. Something got to give!"

Seconds after Shawn hung up, Mo walked in asking, "what's up, you look beat man."

Anger roared from Shawn's voice as he spoke in rage. "You wanna know what's up, I'll tell you what's up. I'm sick and tired of people dying on that bullshit in my center. This place is designed to keep people off drugs, not keep'em on drugs. Do you realize this is the second death, not to mention in just six damn months? I just don't get it anymore. I mean I don't knock no man for what he do to get his hustle on, but don't bring it here. I work my ass off trying to help these people come back to their right frame of mind, and someone come along and destroy what I work my ass off for. I'm not having it, it's not fair. Now you tell me Mo what's up?"

"Mo folded his arms. "I know how you feel man. Look why don't you take the rest of the day off, go home, and get you some rest."

"I got'ah lot'uv work to catch up on, I'll be okay. What about you Mo? How you feeling about all of this cause it seems to me none of this has affected you at all!"

"O' it affects me, but I just don't see anything I can do to stop what's happening. I mean we have over four hundred patients in here, and they all know why they're here. If they put it in their minds' to keep on doing that shit, then the hell with them, because there is no way we can keep up with every move they make day after day. We show them movie after movie about what that shit do to the brain, and they still wanna use that stuff. Come on... man, give me a break. We try, and that's all we can do. Now don't let that happen to those two girls that got the best of your mind. All you can do is your job, and you do that very well. Now please, for me, go home and get some rest man. I'll finish up here."

Yeah, I guess you're right. I do give this place to much of my time. I know it may sound strange, but at times I feel like I'm the victim."

"You just go on home and get you some rest, relax yourself!"

"Are you sure you can handle things here?"

"Of course I can. Sure, I'll be fine."

"Well I'll see you tomorrow. Call me if anything comes up." Shawn headed towards the door and turned around. "Thanks Mo, I appreciate this."

Mo smiled, "that's what friends are for."

Mo made sure Shawn was out of sight and quickly dotted to the phone calling his connection. The phone ringed twice before anyone answered, "hello."

"Yeah this Mo put Bobby on the phone."

"This is Bobby."

Mo's voice turned to rage. "Yes what the fuck you putting in this shit? Another girl od'd today and it ain't no fucking coincidence. Now I wanna know what's in this shit, and I wanna know right now!"

"Okay my brother, calm down man. Look, me and the fellaz put a little strychnine in the dope."

Mo was shocked. "You what? Mothafucka, don't you know a drop of that shit destroy the brain."

"Well it ain't killed nobody so far."

"You stupid son-of-a-bitch! That's why I'm calling your dumb ass now. Two girls done died from using that shit. Man I thought you told me you had the best stuff in town. To make a long story short, I'm through fucking with you so I advise you to take that shit you're selling somewhere else," Mo slammed the phone down hanging it up.

Gena heard a car pulling in the driveway and said, "who can this be?" Ding dong, the bell sounded off. Gena peeked through the peek hole and screamed out. "O my God its Paula," she opened the door. "Girl... look at you, come on in here."

They hugged each other tight as Paula said, "surprise," smiling.

"You look terrific. Now who is this nice looking gentleman?"

"I'm sorry girl, this is Leonard, Leonard this is my girl Gena Montero."

Leonard was five foot, nine inches, dark brown eyes, wavy black hair, medium built, middle thirties.

Leonard smiled, "nice to meet you."

"Nice to meet you too; any friend of Paula's is a friend of mine."

"Paula cut her off, "where is Shawn?"

"He's at work. I can't believe my eyes. Look at you, I'm so glad to see you. When did you get out? Oops, my bag."

"Oh, its okay girl. Leonard already know about that."

Gena smiled, "can I get you guys something to drink?"

"Chile yes, get me something sweet."

"Now bout you Leonard, would you like something to drink?"

"Sure, do you have any beer around?"

"Yepp, but Coors' only."

"Coors' will be fine with me."

Paula smiled, "where's the baby?"

Gena laughed, "girl I almost forgot about him. He's sleep I hope. I'll show'em to you, but first let me get you guys something to drink."

After Gena served the drinks she quickly rushed upstairs to check on the baby. Antonio was awake when she got to him.

"O' you poor thing. How long mommy baby been woke? Come with mommy, your Aunt Paula wanna see you."

Paula smiled as Gena got closer to her with the baby. "Oooh isn't he a doll. Hey there handsome. Can I hold'em?" Gena handed her the baby. "Girl he's so healthy. I see his birthmark is right under his right eye."

"Yeahhh girl, it's a sign letting us know Antonio is in him. I just hope he don't have his daddy attitude; I'm just happy he's a normal child. I know you heard about the accident."

Paula was too busy playing with the baby not really paying Gena any attention. "Hey lil-man, hi there, this your Aunt Paula. Oh he's so cute Gena."

"Paula you never did answer my question; when did you get out the hospital?"

"Actually it's been about two weeks. I'd say a week and five days. I told Shawn not to tell you. I wanted to surprise you," she smiled.

"You most definitely done that, I'm very surprised, and I'm happy. Since you're out you can help me get into my custom-made wedding dress."

"I'll be glad to help you girlfriend. After all that's what friends are for. So how does it feel to be a mother?"

"Wonderful, all but the getting up in the middle of the night, but I'm getting use to it now, thank God."

Leonard interrupted, "excuse me ladies, Gena I think somebody is trying to open your door."

"That must be Shawn, but he supposed to be at work. Let me see who this is at my front door."

Before Gena could get to the door, Shawn was stepping in. Gena kissed him and said, "hi honey, you're home early."

"Yeahhh thanks to Mo. He told me take the rest of the day off; He goin finish up for me today. I see we got company."

Paula smiled, "hi Shawn surprised to see me?"

"No not really."

Gena smiled, "sweetheart this is Leonard, Paula's friend."

"Nice to meet you Leonard."

"Nice to meet you to Shawn. I heard a lot about you."

"All good things I hope," Shawn smiled.

"Paula tells me you the best doctor they have at the center."

"Why thank you Paula, do you remember Missy?"

"Yeah I do, that's my girl."

"Well I have bad news; she od'd today, she's dead."

Paula was shocked, "Lord have mercy, how did it happen?"

"Somebody gave her some bad dope; that's all I know!"

Paula's face turned bitter as she turned to look at Gena thinking to herself, "I know who it is; should I say something to Shawn about it?"

Gena interrupted, "come on you guys let's not spoil a happy day."

Shawn sat down, "you know, come to think about it, the only one who hasn't taken these deaths too serious is Mo. I can't see how he stays so calm; I wish I had that kind'ah mind."

Gena thought to herself, "no you don't. Mo is a no good bastard, and as soon as we get married I'm goin put an end to his career. I'll talk to Paula first; I'm sure she want mind since she's no longer there."

Shawn said, "why don't you guys spend the night with us. We can watch television all night, and talk about the good-o-days."

Paula smiled, "that's cool with me."

Shawn looked at Leonard, "how bout you Leonard, spend the night with us."

"If it's okay with you."

"Sure it's okay; Gena and I can use some company. We ain't had the chance to really go anywhere. Let me get you another beer. I don't know about you Leonard, but I love my beer. Coors' my favorite beer, I'll be right back."

While Shawn was busy getting the beer, Gena said, "well Paula, let me show you where you goin be sleeping. Follow me."

When the two of them reached the top of the stairs Gena said, "girl you know we goin have to do something about Mo!"

"Yeah you're right, we do!"

Gena seemed at ease with Paula's response. "We'll wait till after the wedding. I don't wanna spoil anything for Shawn right now. We'll teach that bastard not to keep on spoiling other people's lives with that shit. Well this is your room right here," Gena opened the door. "You like it?"

Paula stared for a second at the furniture. "Yeah girl it's lovely."

As Gena and Paula were coming back down the stairs, Shawn's eyes were glued on Paula's body as he thought to himself. "Damnn she got'ah body on her; I bet she got some good pussy. I ain't never slept with a black woman before; I sure would like to see what's under them jeans she's wearing."

Gena interrupted his thought saying, "I was showing Paula where they would be sleeping." Shawn didn't hear her speaking; still in a trace from thinking about Paula. "Shawn darling, are you okay?"

Shawn quickly snapped out of it. "O yeah sorry, I'm fine. I was kind'ah daydreaming about something."

"What were you dreaming about?"

"Shawn quickly made up a lie, and said to himself, "if you only knew. I was just thinking about Missy, that's all. She's been on my mind."

An hour passed by and midnight took its toll. Gena stood up from the sofa yarning. "I don't know about you guys, but it's bedtime for me."

Shawn yarned, "yeah me too. We'll see y'all in the morning, goodnight."

An hour and a half passed by before Paula and Leonard decided to retire. Paula watched Leonard get in the bed and said, "I'll be right back baby, I got'ah fresh'n up right quick."

As Paula walked toward the bathroom she could hear that Gena and Shawn were still up. Paula crept to their door and put her ear up against it, and all she could hear was, "yes Shawn, yess, yess, oooh, oooh, that feel good, yesss, yes."

After listening to Gena and Shawn make love, Paula got hot between the legs and said to herself while walking to the bathroom, "Leonard goin give me the same treatment. Damn, the way Shawn putting it on Gena makes me wish I was in her shoes right about now."

A new day set in; Gena was the first to awake. She went downstairs to prepare breakfast. Minutes later Shawn woke and joined her downstairs for a cup of coffee.

Gena smiled, "well good morning. How do you feel this morning?"

"Baby I feel terrific, how bout you, how do you feel?"

"Sore as….hell, other than that, I feel like a queen. You know it's been awhile since I had sex with a man, but I admit, you were damn good sweetheart."

Paula burst through the kitchen door. "Good morning you two; Leonard will be down shortly, he's in the bathroom washing up. So Mr. Bomoski you up mighty early. What time you got'ah be to work today?"

"You know me Paula, I really don't have a certain time, but to answer your question, I decided to take today off. After all tomorrow is the big day; ain't that right hunny?"

She smiled, "that's right."

Paula sighed, "stupid old me, I forgot today is the last day in March."

Leonard walked in, "how's everybody this morning?"

They all spoke back at the same time. Shawn sipped his coffee saying, "Leonard do you like to fish?"

"I love fishing."

"Well how bout you and I go do a little fishing this morning. That's if you don't have anything else planned."

"Nothing at all, I'd love too."

"Good, that'll give the girls time to catch up on their lost time. I'm sure they have a lot to talk about. In the meantime you and I can get to know each other better."

They sat around the table talking until Leonard and Shawn finally took off for fishing.

Paula started laughing out of the blue, Gena smiled. "What you laughing at silly?"

"I'm laughing at you girl, I been thinking about this all morning and girl I got to say something about it."

Gena smiled, "what are you talking about?"

"I'm talking about you and Shawn. I heard you two going at it last night. Girl you sounded like you ain't never had no dick before. I mean you sounded like'ah virgin. He was wearing that little man in the boat out. Made my stuff hot; I had to geek Leonard up after hearing you two going at it like mad minks."

"Actually I felt like'ah virgin. It's been a long time for me you know."

"Yeah… girl I know."

"But girl, the feeling; girl it felt so damn good."

Paula smiled, "I just know it did. I started to come and join in the bed with y'all. That's how hot I had got between these legs."

Paula was serious, but said it in a jokingly way. Gena looked into her eyes saying, "why didn't you?"

"Girl if I would'ah came in that room while you two were getting it on, you'll still be choking my ass."

"I would'nah done no such thing so next time don't hesitate just come on in."

As Gena walked away Paula said to herself, "is this woman serious or what? She just don't know I'll suck that spur tongue out her pussy. I'm goin crash on her one day. She don't know I go both ways. I should crack on'er now; I'll just wait for the right moment. Who knows, maybe she wants me as bad as I want her. After she did tell me how much she admired my body, and now that I think about it she could go both ways. O'well, if she do it'll come out."

Gena yelled out from the kitchen. "Paula check on the baby for me please!"

She shouted out, "sure, I'm on my way."

When Paula got to the baby she found him playing with his rattler. "Hey there little-fellow. Hi… It's your Aunt Paula again. Your mommy getting married tomorrow; we goin dress you up so you can look handsome for aunt' tee. Come on let's go see what mommy doing."

As Paula walked down the stairs she made up her mind to test Gena saying to herself, "I know what I'll do; when I take the baby to'er I'm goin walk right up to'er and kiss her on the back of her neck with my tongue. See how she responds to that!"

Gena was still washing dishes; Paula walked up to her with the baby still in her arms, slid her tongue across the back of Gena's neck and walked away.

Gena stood still for a minute and said to herself, "I wonder what's on her mind? Well I'm fix'n to find out in a few seconds. She don't know I'm already attracted to her ass; I like women too. Let me go see what's up with her, and I know just how I'm goin play'er too."

Paula was sitting on the sofa holding the baby when Gena came up behind her and leaned over and put her tongue in Paula's mouth.

Paula held the baby to the side saying, "girl I been praying for this moment."

Gena smiled, "so have I so you see we really do need each other, as I'm goin make you feel like no one has ever made you feel before. Now you just take off them clothes and lay your sweet self down on this carpet. I'm goin give you something you can't get from no one," they undressed.

And what's that?" They continue undressing.

"Another woman, and you can take them candy colored panties off too, I want all of you."

Gena made sure the baby was comfortable and continued taking her clothes off. Once she was done undressing she got on her knees and put her mouth between Paula's legs gently using her tongue to caress the hairs between Paula's legs, working her way to the spur tongue.

"Oooh Gena that feels good. Suck that pussy, yeahhh suck it."

Minutes later, Paula burst. Quickly she got up pushing Gena backward letting her titties run up and down Gena's stomach, and sliding down placing her tongue in Gena already wet pussy.

"Yes Paula, ahh yeah, such that pussy, yeah, yesss, yess, suck it, suck that pussy. Damn you know how to make it feel good. I'm cumming, I'm cumming, ahhh!" Gena came. "Girl you make me feel better than any man could. We're made for each other. Quick girl let's get dressed before somebody walk in on us. Damn that felt good. You got'ah promise me something."

"And what's that?"

"Promise me you'll never leave me!"

"I promise I'll never leave you! You know tomorrow is your day; you'll be a married woman."

"Yeah I know. I'm just doing what I think is best for my son and I think I'm doing the right thing!"

"Of course you are, and besides I think you and Shawn make a lovely couple. I'm happy for you."

"There's only one thing Paula."

"And what's that?"

"He can't make me feel the way you make me feel."

"I know girl, but no-one can never find out about us. This is our little secret!"

"You're right; no one must ever find out, my lips are sealed. Now come on girl! Let's take a quick shower together before they get here. I'll fix the baby a fresh bottle and put him in his crib while you and I have just'ah lil-bit more fun."

After Gena and Paula were done getting each other off in the shower, they went downstairs to wait on Shawn and Leonard.

Two hours later Shawn and Leonard came walking through the door. Shawn held a string full of fish in his left hand. Gena looked at all the fish and smiled.

"It looks like you two caught all the fish in Lake Michigan so I assume we having fish for dinner?"

Shawn smiled, "yeah if we can find somebody to clean them."

Leonard laughed. "Everybody just relax, I'll do the cleaning. It's the least I can do for you two. Y'all just consider it a wedding gift from me."

Gena and Shawn laughed. Shawn said, "Leonard is a funny guy, I enjoyed his company today."

Leonard thought to himself, "I don't know what y'all laughing about. Yeah, a wedding gift, cause I ain't got jack shit to give you. Now laugh at that you two ignorant motherfuckaz. If I did have some money I wouldn't waste it on y'all rich asses anyway. I'm the one who need a gift," he smiled. "Where's Paula?"

"She went upstairs to take a nap. She said last night was a long night if you know what I mean."

Shawn answered the door, "hello."

"What happened to you today man?"

"Well Mo, I decided to take today off. I knew you had everything under control back there."

"Yeah everything is fine here. I just called to see if you was all right. I'll see you tomorrow on your big day, talk to you later."

After Shawn hung up Gena asked, "who was that honey?"

"That was Mo checking up on us, wanting to know why I wasn't at work today. I forgot to tell'em I went fishing. O'well maybe it wasn't meant for him to know."

"I hope you stopped by the store on your way home."

"Damn sweetheart, I sure didn't. I'm just kidding we did stop by the store."

"Did you get my you know what?"

"Yeah, but I hope it's not that time of the month yet."

"It's not, but I still like to have'm around just in case it happen earlier then what I expect."

"As long as it don't happen on our wedding day."

"I don't expect it to happen for at least another week. I'm glad Paula goin watch the baby for us tomorrow while we go celebrate."

Shawn smiled, "Yeah me too, that's sweet of her to do that for you."

As the night grew old, Shawn and Gena were the first to turn-in, leaving Paula and Leonard downstairs watching television.

The next day Gena was the first to wake as usual. She stretched and yarned. "Oh thank you God for another day. In a few hours I will be a married woman. I can remember when Antonio and I got married; it was so beautiful. Now here I am taking that vow again. I better wake everybody up. We ain't got but'ah few hours before it's three o'clock."

"Shawn, Shawn darling wake up."

Shawn mumbled, "I'm up."

"Good, I'll put your coffee on."

When Gena got downstairs Paula was already in the kitchen making breakfast. Gena walked up to her and put her arms around her and hissed her lips quickly.

Paula gazed into Gena's eyes and smiled, "congratulations girlfriend."

"Thanks, and don't forget what I told you, I need you Paula."

"I need you too, and don't you forget our little secret. What time is the preacher supposed to get here?"

"He's supposed to be here around three and I wanna be fully dressed by then, and that's when you come into the picture."

"Don't worry girl I'll have you in that gown in no time."

"As the clock ticked, Shawn was getting dressed in his room while Gena got dressed in Paula's room.

Leonard had the door under control; people started popping in by the minutes.

Shawn arranged everything for the wedding, from the live band to the flowers.

After Paula zipped Gena's dress, Gena smiled.

"Paula you grab the baby while I take one last look in the mirror at myself. Well it's that time and the clock in here say's five too."

Leonard yelled upstairs, "the reverend here y'all got'ah come on."

"We're coming," Gena yelled.

"How do I look Paula?"

"You look lovely girl, now come on here. Let's get downstairs before everybody decides to leave."

Paula went downstairs first with the baby and took a seat next to Leonard.

Gena stood at the top of the steps for a minute listening to the band play (here comes the bride.)

As Gena started walking down the stairs, she made eye contact with Shawn and started smiling.

Shawn was dressed in a powder-blue tuxedo. Mo also wore the same color tuxedo. They even had the baby dressed in blue.

The organ stop playing; silence set in as the preacher began the ceremony.

"Dear relatives and friends, we are gathered here today to join this lovely couple together. Is there anyone who thinks these two should not be joined together, speak now or forever hold your peace?"

Gena looked over at Paula and smiled thinking to herself, "Paula seems so happy for me."

The Reverend smiled, "do you Gena take this man to be your husband? To love, to cherish until death do you apart?"

She smiled, "I do!"

"I now pronounce you two man and wife. You may kiss the bride."

After they kissed, Shawn smiled. "How does it feel being Mrs. Bomoski?"

"Like a dream come true, I love you!"

"I love you more Mrs. Bomoski! We better make sure our guests know where the reception goin be."

Shawn got on the microphone. "Excuse, excuse me ladies and gentlemen." Everyone got quiet. "The reception is downtown at the Renaissance on the twenty-third floor. I hope to see y'all face in the place and for you my lovely bride, I have a surprise waiting for you when we get there."

Paula and Leonard watched Gena and Shawn get into the powder blue limousine.

As soon as Gena took her seat she smiled. "May I ask what surprise you have for me darling?"

"No, you may not, just wait and see."

The limousine driver pulled up to the front entrance, got out, and opened the door for the newlyweds. He too was dressed in powder blue.

Shawn gives the driver a hundred a hundred dollar tip and smiled saying, "thank you my man. You're welcome to come in if you like. If not, see you around ten."

The limousine driver was thirty-two years old, light blue eyes, thin built, and clean shaved. "Thank you for the invitation sir, but I think I'll pass on this one. You two enjoy yourselves; I'll be here at your service when you guys are ready to leave. Good day sir."

When Gena and Shawn made it to the twenty-third floor, Gena couldn't believe her eyes. Her favorite group *The Temptations* was performing.

Gena smiled. "Oh my God Shawn, no you didn't."

"Yes I did."

"I can't believe it, this is a surprise. *The Temptations* are my favorite singers. Can you introduce me to them?"

"I sure can, I know all of them."

"Ohhh Shawn, I'm excited!"

Gena's body began moving to the beat of the music as she said, "dance with me."

They started dancing, "you can really dance honey," she smiled.

"Thank you, I didn't know I had it in me, Elvis was my teacher," they laughed.

"Well, I can see he taught you well."

"Your pretty good yourself, who taught you?"

"I taught myself."

"You did good. Soon as they finish playing this song I'll introduce you to the fellaz."

After *The Temptations* were done performing that song, one of *The Temptations* named Melvin spotted Shawn on the dance floor and told David, "Shawn is here man."

David spoke through the microphone, "come on up here Shawn, we see you out there trying to do the boogaloo."

Shawn waved his hand. "Come on baby, here's your chance to meet your favorite singers."

Shawn took Gena on stage, "what's up fellaz, I'd like y'all to meet my lovely wife Gena."

One at a time they introduced themselves and when they were done introducing themselves, Melvin said in his deep voice, "we'd like to dedicate this next song to you two."

Gena smiled, "I can't wait to hear it. I love you guys' music. I want all y'all to know you guys are my favorite singers in the world when it comes to singing songs."

David smiled, "we know, your husband told us when he got in touch with us and don't want to long to look us up man. You know you still our main man. Now you tow just grab something to sip on and relax this song is for you two." They started singing (when a man loves a woman.)

While The Temptations were busy singing, Leonard was busy snooping around in Shawn's bedroom. Leonard searched each dresser-draw, worked his way to the closet, and went through each suit-coat finding nothing. After searching each suit-coat, he slid them to the side spotting another inside the closet.

After spotting the door he said, "bingo, its got'a be something in this room he's trying to hide. This door is in a very unusual place. Let's take a look behind door number two." He opened the door and couldn't believe his eyes.

"Well I'll be damned. This man has enough artillery in here to hold back the national guards. I ain't never seen one man with so many guns. I believe he's into more than the doctor business. Well… what do you know; a picture of

Shawn and the man himself. Long time no see Sorcerer; we been trying to buss your no good ass for centuries. No one seemed to be able to get close enough to your smooth ass. I remember you putting the hit on Montero, your own man. You did quite a number on his boys too that night. You're a dangerous motha-fucka that's for sure. I can't see myself having anything to do with you, but I guess teach his own. I hope Shawn ain't tied up with yoe know good ass. If he is I'm goin have to put'ah end to his career too."

Leonard was careful not to touch anything as he slid the clothing back in place, quietly shutting the closet door back and headed downstairs to join Paula and the baby.

Paula cleared her throat, "what you been doing all that time upstairs?"

"I just been picking up here and there in the guess room. You know baby, when I first met you I knew you was the one for me, especially after you told me you had a friend that stays in Bloomfield Hills. When you said her name was Gena Montero I knew without a doubt she was probably rich and famous."

Leonard went into a deep thought. "Yeahhh the name Gena Montero; I knew she had to be the wife of the legend Antonio Montero. Thank you for leading me to her. Gena is the spoiled type; she loves men with lots of money. That's the only reason that bitch married Shawn. If Paula knew I was a detective she'd blow my cover. She thinks I'm a landscaper. This case has just begun and I owe all the thanks to you Paula."

Paula interrupts the thought with a push on his shoulder, "yeah baby."

"I been talking my ass off and you ain't heard'ah word I said."

"I'm sorry baby I was dazed, you know in a deep thought, I'm back now."

After the reception, Shawn had the driver to cruise around Belle-Isle before taking them back to the house. After a few glasses of champagne, Gena was in the mood for love. "Make love to me Shawn." Shawn quickly closed the curtains and after twenty minutes of love-making, Shawn opened the curtain back and said to the limousine driver, "to the house."

The limousine driver turned his head toward Shawn, hoping he could catch a quick glimpse of Gena naked and said to himself, "damn she got her dress on."

Five minutes later, the driver was pulling into the drive-way saying, "well sir we're here." He got out and opened the door of the limousine for them.

Gena smiled and said to the driver, "You can come in and have a drink if you like, we not goin kidnap you. We just got'ah grab a few things, then we're off to the airport and that's where we say good-night to you."

When they got inside the house no one was in sight, Gena yelled, "we're back!" Paula comes downstairs. "Girl, you won't believe who I met at the reception tonight. Girl, I met all of the Temptations, every last one of them."

Paula smiled, "The Temptations."

"Yeah honey, *The Temptations*. Now you got enough pampers and milk to supply every child in Michigan. We'll be gone about seven days."

"Girl is that all, I want even know you was gone."

Shawn went upstairs to get the luggage ad his favorite sports-coat, and when he opened the closet door the first thing came out of his mouth. "Damn, somebody been in my room snooping around. Why would anybody come in here moping around? Fuck it let me grab this luggage and get the hell out of here. Wait a minute; I better check my private room out first then I'll get the hell out of here. There's only one way I'll know for sure if anybody been in there. I'll check the doorknob for prints, then I'm out of here."

Shawn took the luggage downstairs to the limousine driver, and then said to Gena, "give me a few more minutes honey, I got one more thing to take care of before we go."

Leonard asked, "what is it Shawn, maybe I can help you out if you want me too."

"That's not necessary Leonard, it'll only take me a second to do this, thanks anyway."

Shawn went to the basement and grabbed his finger-print kit and the camera. Leonard could see Shawn carrying the camera upstairs and said to himself, "oh, he fix'n to take plenty of pictures."

Shawn dusted the doorknob for prints and said, "somebody was definitely in here!" He snapped a picture of the prints. "Damn, I'm glad I keep this doorknob spotless. Gena could'ah went in there, but she would've questioned me by now about the door. I'll have the prints ran off when I get to Vegas, and I hope they belong to the right person, God knows I do!"

"Finally," Gena said as she watched Shawn come down the stairs.

"Well, I'm ready baby," Shawn said looking at his watch.

Gena kissed the baby and hugged Paula. Paula whispered in her ear, "I love you."

"I love you too," she whispered. "See you guys when we get back."

When they got in the limousine, Shawn said, "I've arranged for my private jet to take us there. My drunk pilot should already be there when we get to the airport."

As soon as the limousine driver opened the door for them, a voice called out, "you whoo."

Shawn smiled, "oh, there he is, you say leave Mr. Limo driver."

"My name is Ron, sir."

"Well Ron, thanks for the service, I'll be in touch, drive careful." Shawn smiled at Mack, "well if ain't old Mack. Good to see you my friend."

"Good to see' ya Shawn."

"Gena this is Mack, Mack this is my lovely wife Gena."

"Nice to meet you ma'am."

"Nice to meet you sir."

"Where to tonight my son?"

"Vegas Mack."

Mack put his hat on, "Vegas here we come."

Gena smiled. "How long you been flying planes Mack?"

"All my life lil-lady; you see my father was my pilot, his father. I guess you can say it runs in the family. Now you two just relax. I'll have you two in Vegas before y'all can say all you're a,b,c's."

When they arrived in Vegas, their first stop was (Hertz-Rent-A-Car.) When they got inside, Gena couldn't believe how everyone seemed to know her husband so well. Voices from everywhere were calling his name. "Hi, Mr. Bomoski, hello Mr. Bomoski, how are you Mr. Bomoski, nice to see you again Mr. Bomoski, long time no see Mr. Bomoski."

Gena had no idea Shawn and Sorcerer practically owned Vegas. A voice came from behind the counter, "why hello Mr. Bomoski, I see your back again."
"Yeah I am and this time with my new wife we got married yesterday."

"Well, congratulations to you both."

"Thank you," Gena said smiling.

Shawn smiled, "is there a phone I can use real quick?"

"You bet there is, you can use this one if you like."

"I'll only be a minute."

Shawn dialed the number, "hello, Sunset Motel, Tara speaking."

"Yeah, this Bomoski, I'm in town and I have someone with me."

"Everything's already set up for you Mr. Bomoski."

"Very good, you have a good day."

Shawn hung up, "well, Gena sweetheart, everything is already set up for us. Now all we have to do is enjoy ourselves and I know just the place to start us off."

Shawn pulled the rented Jaguar in front of the casino. The valet escorted the two of them into the casino and once they got inside all Gena could hear was Shawn's name being called all over the casino.

They were seated at a candle lit table. The waited smiled, "hi Mr. Bomoski, what can I get for you and your lady friend?"

"Terri, this is my wife, and you can bring us a bottle of the best champagne in the house."

"Anything else Mr. Bomoski?" The waiter asked smiling.

"Yeah, this is your table for as long as I'm in town. Give my wife whatever she wants while I go and make this very important phone call."

"Whatever you say Mr. Bomoski, I'll start right now. What would you like to eat Mrs. Bomoski?" Shawn left to make his call, "You have a very nice husband Mrs. Bomoski. You're very lucky to have a man like Shawn for a husband."

"Yes, I know," Gena's mind drifted back to Antonio. "I remember when Antonio brought me to this same casino. He treated me like I wasn't shit one night in here; it was so embarrassing. I said I wasn't never goin set foot in a gambling casino again after what he did to me."

Shawn shuts the door to his office and called his buddy Captain Redge. The phone rang three times. "Captain Redge speaking, homicide and narcotics division."

"Yeah Captain, this Bomoski."

"Bomoski, what' ah surprise. What can a man like me do for a man like you?"

"I need you to run some prints for me. You want me to meet you somewhere; I'm at my office at the casino."

"I'll be there in an hour."

"See you when you get here."

Shawn went back downstairs to join his wife. "Hi sweetheart, you enjoying yourself?"

"Yes I am did you make your call?"

"Yeah and he should be here in about an hour. In the meantime let's enjoy ourselves. After all this is our honeymoon. Are you hungry?"

"Yeah, I was waiting on you to get back before I ordered me anything."

Tara came to the table and took their orders. "What would you guys like?"

Gena smiled. "I'll have the lobster dipped in butter sauce."

"I'll have the same."

Tara smiled, "would y'all like something to drink with the lobsters?"

"Yes," Gena said, "bring me a scotch and coke on the rocks."

"I'll have the same."

Right in the middle of their dinner Shawn spots Captain Redge. "Excuse me for a second honey, this won't take long."

Shawn took the Captain upstairs to his office. "Now what can I do for you Bomoski?"

"I want you to take these prints and get me a name on these ASAP."

"Where did you get these prints from?"

"I got them from the doorknob to my private room at my house back in Detroit. Somebody been moping around in our business; with the business we're in we can't afford to take no chances!"

"I'll get right on it. I'll have a name for you tomorrow, don't worry, take care. I'll see you tomorrow. Oh, one more thing."

"What's that captain?"

"Congratulations, I'm sorry I didn't make it to the wedding, I'll meet the misses tomorrow."

"Yeah, see you tomorrow Captain."

Shawn saw the Captain off and went to join Gena. She was busy counting her winnings when he got to her. "Oh, I see you had the lucky coin. How much did you win?"

"I will say about four thousand. Let's leave now. I have a jackpot that needs to be hit, if you know what I mean."

Shawn smiled, "I'll have the car brought around."

Twenty minutes later they were inside their room at the Sunset Motel. For hours they made passionate love.

Gena fell asleep on Shawn's chest and seconds later Shawn dozed off. As they slept the night away, daybreak had finally set in.

They were awakened by the room service lady. Shawn could hear the lady's voice telling the people next to them, "clean up time, room service!"

Shawn touched Gena, "wake up baby, rise and shine."

"Ohhh Shawn, I got'ah hang over."

Shawn laughed. "Ah hang over, would you like to join me in the shower?"

"I sure would darling."

Shawn picked her up and carried her into the bathroom where they made love in the shower as the warm water bounced off their bodies.

Gena moaned in passion until they heard the knock on the door, Gena sighed. "Who could that be?"

"I don't know, but I better go see. We wouldn't want the clean-up lady to walk in on us while we're making out in the shower."

Shawn wrapped the towel around his wet body and went to the door. "Who is it?"

It's me, the Captain."

Shawn quickly unlocked the door. "How did you know I was here?"

"You know a man in my line of work got to keep with every man in my county. Anyway I came to give you

93

that information you wanted on them prints. Is it okay to talk here?"

Gena walks out the bathroom wearing a silk blue robe. "Captain Redge, this is my wife Gena and Gena this is Captain Redge."

"Nice to meet you Gena."

"Pleased to meet you Captain Redge."

"So how are you enjoying your stay here in Vegas?"

"I'm enjoying every minute of it."

"That's good, so Somoski is it okay to talk here or what?"

"Well Captain, Gena and I were just on our way back to the casino. You can meet me at my office there."

"Fine, I'll meet you there. Oh, once again, it's a pleasure meeting you Gena."

Gena smiled, "I'll see you at the casino captain, good day."

"Good day to you both."

As soon as the Captain left Gena said, "what is so confidential Shawn that you can't share it with your wife?"

"I don't wanna lie to you Gena so please try to understand. It's nothing for you to worry about. I'm just taking care of a little business while I'm here. Me and the captain go back a long way and he's just helping me protect my investments. There, are you satisfied now? I just want you to be happy Gena. Don't worry about me okay?"

"Okay, if you say so, I just don't wanna see anything happen to you that's all. I love you!"

"Don't worry; I can handle myself very well in this neck of the woods."

Shawn pulled Gena to his body and kissed her. They got dressed and drove back to the casino, where they would spend most of their day gambling. They sat at the same table and had the same waitress, Tara.

Shawn spotted Sammy Davis Jr. and smiled. "There go Sammy Davis Jr. baby. He comes here every week to do some serious betting. I'll introduce you to him, but first let me take care of a little business with the captain."

Before Shawn could get out his seat the captain was standing right behind him saying, "hello again Gena."

"Hello Captain Redge."

Shawn downed his drink, "let's go to the office."

"Fine with me."

Once they got in the office Shawn said, "all right Captain, do we have a name?"

"Yes we do."

"Good, who is it?"

"These prints belong to Leonard Boston."

"Leonard Boston, that son-of-a-bitch."

"That's the good news I just gave you; the bad news is this Boston character is a private investigator. He works for the homicide and narcotics team."

Shawn went into a rage, "that mothafucka; how dare that cheap, low-down mothafucka come into my house and invade my privacy. I want you to contact Sorcerer, tell'em to send me two of his best hit-men to Detroit. Tell'em to have them at my office at the Millender Center in four days. You got that?"

"Yeah I got it."

"I want this bitch dead as soon as possible. I can't believe this shit; this punk ass nigga is staying at my house right now."

"I'm out of here, consider my job done. I'll take care of everything soon as I get back to head-quarters."

"One more thing Captain."

"What's that?"
"Tell Sorcerer not to worry, I got everything under control."

"I'll be sure to tell'em that. I'll contact you later on."

"You do that, I'm depending on you."

Shawn joined Gena. "Sorry it took me so long, everything's taken care of."

"That's good, now maybe you can introduce me to Sammy."

"Oh yeah, I almost forgot. Come on let's go find him, he's in here somewhere, probably at the black-jack table." He spotted Sammy, "bingo, there he is at the black-jack table as usual."

They walked up to Sammy. "Hello Mr. Davis, long time no see."

Sammy smiled, "Mr. Bomoski, what'ah pleasant surprise. Want you join me in a game Mr. Bomoski?"

"Actually, Mr. Davis, I came over to introduce you to my wife."

"Wife," he said smiling.

"Yeahh wife, this is Mrs. Bomoski."

"My pleasure Mrs. Bomoski."

"It's a pleasure meeting you Mr. Davis. I'm a big fan of yours."

"Why don't you two join me for a couple'uv games?"

"Why we would love too?"

"How long are you two love birds staying in Vegas?"

97

Gena smiled, "we're leaving on the fifth."

"That's good, I'm sure I'll see you two again before you guys take off."

"I'm sure you will Mr. Davis, "she said taking her last sip out the glass.

"Would you two like something to drink?"

Shawn smiled, "we already have a table set up. Perhaps you'll join me and my wife for brunch."

"I would love too." While Shawn and Gena were busy entertaining Sammy, Leonard was back in Detroit playing detective.

Leonard scanned through Shawn's telephone book and said to himself, "Shawn has connections all right. One of these numbers got'ah be Sorcerer's." Leonard put the phone book in his pocket. "I'll hold on to this; it can come in handy. I'm gone put an end to them drug-dealing bastards and Shawn goin lead me to the big fish."

Leonard laid next to Paula. "Leonard, how long you been landscaping?"

"About fifteen years now, why you ask?"

"Well, I was just thinking maybe you could ask Shawn to hire you to do their lawn. I'm sure he would pay you good."

"I wish I would, but the crew I work with only works in the suburb area. We don't never come this far out.

Besides, with the kind of money Shawn makes, he probably already got lawn service."

"Well, I was just trying to look out for you."

"Thanks anyway baby."

"Look who's up Leonard," she smiled.

"Oh, boy I know he's hungry. He's been sleep all day. Auntie goin feed that baby, yes she is."

"While you're making his bottle, bring me back a beer please."

When Paula left to go warm up the baby's bottle, Leonard got straight on the telephone. "Yes, I would like to make a collect call."

"Your name and number please?"

"Boston, 235-1335."

The operator put the call through and the voice on the end said, "Boston man, where the hell are you?"

Leonard spoke quickly, "listen to me; I want you to run the name Shawn Bomoski through the computer. I know I'm on to something big."

"Hold on, it'll only take a minute."

Two minutes later, "yeah man, the computer says Shawn Bomoski is a doctor, works at a rehabilitation center, and has no criminal record. The man is legit."

"Okay thanks man for your time," Leonard hung the phone up. "Damn it got'ah be something on this dude connecting him to Sorcerer's drug enterprises. Unless he's working under an alias name, and that could well much be. I'll just have to find out a little more about this so called doctor Bomoski."

Paula walked in asking, "who was that on the phone?"

"That was moms. I called to see how she was doing."

"You just reminded me, I got to call my mama too. I'll call'er after I finish the baby, wit his fat-self."

"You do that, I'm sure she'll be happy to hear your voice." Leonard thought to himself, "yeah, that'll give me time to go through the rest of this crooked-son-of-a-bitch things."

After Paula was done feeding the baby, she held him in one arm while she dialed the number to her mother's house.

Leonard ran upstairs when he heard her talking. "Hi, mama, it's your baby."

Smiling, "girl, I know who this is. Where you at? You know you could at least call and eheck on your son more often than you do."

"How is he mama?"

"He's fine, getting bigger by the minute and talk about bad. Girl, he's the ringleader," Sharen laughed. "I miss you Paula, I wish you would come on home. Come spend some time with your son."

"Mama he don't even know me."

"That's because you want giv'em a chance to get to know you, shit. I barely know you. You keep popping in and out of his life. What do you expect?" Tears start falling from her eyes.

"Your right mama, I'll be down there in a few days. I'm watching a friend of mine baby until they come back from their honeymoon."

"You can watch somebody else baby, but you can't watch your own baby? What kind'ah shit is that?"

"Don't start mama they should be back any day now. When they get back I'll be to see you and my son. Where's he now?"

"He's outside playing with the kids across the street."

"Well tell'em I said hi and that I love'em. I guess I'll let you go. I just wanted to hear your voice, I love you mama," tears began falling from her eyes.

"I love you to baby, talk to you later, you take care of yourself."

Paula hung up the phone and wiped the tears from her eyes.

Meanwhile back to Shawn and Gena in Vegas. "Gena, darling in a few minutes your bout to see the funniest man in the world come on stage. I'll give you one guess who it is."

"Okay then, Redd Foxx."

Shawn laughed. "Nope, it's not Redd Foxx," he said still laughing.

"Who then?"

"Richard Pryor."

"Now why didn't I know that? He is the funniest man in the world. I can't wait to see him."

"Neither can I."

As they were talking the announcer grabbed the microphone saying, "ladies and gentlemen, put your hands together for the funniest man in the world. I present to you, Mr. Richarddddd, Pryorrrr."

The crowd went crazy as they watched Richard grab the microphone.

Richard spotted Shawn sitting out in the audience and said, "I see we have Mr. Bomoski in the house. Shawn, my main man, good to see you in the house today."

Gena looked at Shawn and said," damn baby, who don't know you? It seems like to me you're the star here in Vegas."

"I just know a lot of people, that's all," he said smiling.

Richard rubbed his mustache. "Since your here Shawn, you make sure you see me after the show." Shawn nodded his head in a yeah motion. "Well, hello out there ladies, gents. Damn, when I seen my main man in the house I liked to forgot all about y'all ass."

The audience was cracking up. "Anybody in here own'ah car? Damn look at the hands go up, I tell you the truth, fat mothafuckas don't need a car. Look at that fat mothafucka sitting in the back there with the gold chain on his forehead. I see why he got it on his forehead, he ain't got no neck."

The audience was laughing out their seats. "You, big boy, yeah you. Don't look like you drove here today. You did! Well what you drive, ah all you can eat truck? Somebody stick'ah hog in that nigga mouth. Who's that woman sitting next to you, talking bout, you can get off my man. You better shut-your-mouth before I have two of them chairs kicked from under yoe fat ass."

Gena laughed saying, "boyyy this man is funny. I got to get this tape."

Shawn smiled, "that's no problem baby. I'm sure my buddy has one backstage somewhere."

After the show, Shawn and Gena went to Richard's dressing room backstage. Richard laughed and said, "damn Shawn, its sure good to see you again. Where you been hiding yourself man?"

"Before I answer that question I want you to meet my wife. This is my wife Gena."

"Pleased to meet you Gena."

"Nice to meet you too, I enjoyed your show."

"Glad you liked it. Now back to you my man."

"I been busy Rich, wait'ah minute, let's get to the point. What can I do for ya Rich?"

Richard whispered in his ear, "I need you to front me a lil-something."

"Here, take this number, tell'em I said to give you what you want, and Rich do be on time this time."

"Don't worry man, I'll have the money back to them in no time and on time. Shit man, this Rich you talking too."

"You're a good man Rich, I'll be seeing you. By the way, you wouldn't happen to have'ah tape of the show around?"

"Sure do right there," Rich pointed at the desk. "Grab you one."

"Thanks Rich!"

"Yeah man, anytime for you my friend, take care man, by the way."

Shawn was just opening the door and turned around saying, "yeah Rich."
Richard smiled, "you got'ah fine ass wife. Don't see what she sees in your ugly ass."

Shawn and Gena laughed, Shawn said," see ya Rich."

When Gena and Shawn left, Richard smiled and said to himself, "now there go one rich son-of-a-bitch, the man ass even shaped like'ah hundred dollar bill."

"Where to now?" Gena asked.

"I arranged for a limousine to pick us up here. It's probably here by now waiting on us. I wanna show you the rest of Vegas."

As the chauffeur drove them around Vegas, Gena thought to herself, "I been through these places many times."

Gena smiled, "Shawn, I remember that restaurant over there. Antonio use to take me there all the time when he was dealing drugs. He never let me meet any of the people he was dealing with in there. I never got the chance to meet his connection. All I did was play the slot machines."

Shawn thought to himself, "if you knew Antonio was going to that restaurant to meet me you'd probably faint. I liked Antonio, he had a lot'ah balls, but he should've stayed loyal to Sorcerer. I can remember plain as day when Sorcerer sent his squad after him. Now I'm married to his beautiful Gena. I know he's turning over in his grave behind that one. O'well sorry Antonio, I got to do the things you didn't do, and that's stay loyal and treat Gena with some respect."

"Shawn, I see you like today drama a lot."

"Yes, but only about you baby."

Gena smiled and laid her head on his chest saying, "I love you Shawn, whatever you're doing just be careful."

"I'm telling you baby there's nothing to worry about."

Gena thought to herself, "yeahhh you have to much pull down here not to be doing nothing, you're into something!"

Shawn interrupted her thoughts. "How bout us having dinner at the restaurant you said you and Antonio went too all the time?"

"Sounds good to me."

"Driver," Shawn called out, "to the Flamingo Diner please."

"I'll have y'all there in no time."
Ten minutes later the driver was pulling in the Flamingo Diner parking lot. Shawn looked at the lights in the parking lot reflecting off the lake and thought back to the time he bought the restaurant a few years ago, but never changed the name of the restaurant.

Shawn said, "see that lake over there Gena; I can remember when Lucky drowned in that same lake we're looking at. It happened on Apploni Luso birthday. Lucky was drinking pretty heavy that night. I remember him stumbling through that door." Pointing to the door of the restaurant, "I thought he was gone home. Still to this day I wish I would'ah walked him to his car. He'd probably still be living today."

"It's not your fault Shawn, things like that happen all the time."

"I know baby, I just don't think his death was an accident. Oh well, that's over and done with, let's go eat, I'm starving.

"Me too."

When they got inside the restaurant, the table was already set up for two. Two candles burned; one on each side of the table with a bottle of the best wine in the house sitting in the middle of the table on ice.

Gena smiled saying, "ohhh Shawn, this is so romantic. You sure do know how to treat'ah lady."

"Not just any lady, my lady." Shawn politely pulled her chair out for her to sit down. "You just sit your lovely self down here while I pop the top on this sherry wine."

Shawn filled her wine glass half-way and did the same thing to his, and smiled saying, "Gena darling, let's toast to a beautiful relationship."

They touched glasses, saying at the same time, "to a beautiful relationship."

Gena smiled saying, "it's my turn now, let's toast to the boogie, boogie."

Shawn laughed as they both said at the same time, "to the boogie, boogie," and touched glasses.

"Shawn sweetheart, I'm having so much fun."

"So am I honey! Now what would you like to eat sweetheart?"

"Waiter," he called out.

The waiter didn't waste any time. "Yesss, what will it be for you two tonight?" She asked smiling.

Shawn stared at the menu and said, "I'll have the today's special."

"And what will you be having miss?" The waiter asked smiling.

"I'll have the same and while you're here could you point me in the direction of the ladies room?"

"Sure, just follow me."

Gena smiled, "I use to know where everything in here was at, but they done changed this place around since the last time I was in here."

When Gena got inside the bathroom she said," damn, sorry Shawn, no more sex for a few days. Mother Nature don't wait on nobody, he'll understand."

When Gena got back to the table, she said, "well Mr. Bomoski, I have…"

Shawn cut her off, "you don't have to say it, let me guess, Mother Nature has finally arrived."

"Your guess is correct, but we want let that get in the way of this dinner."

"Of course not, here, let me pour you another drink. You know Gena, I want you to know what I do on the side for a living, but right now isn't the right time sweetheart."

"I know you do, but I think I already know, so when you're ready to sit down and talk about it, let me know!"

"I will tell you this much about me, I have entirely too much money; so much I barely know what to do with it."

Gena grabbed his hand and held it. "Don't worry about money Shawn; you have to enjoy life while you can. Just answer one more thing for me."

"What's that baby?"

"If you have so much money why do you work?"

"I work because I'm an educated man and I enjoy doing what I do. Another thing, I own that rehabilitation center and a couple more in different states. Hell, I even own this restaurant here." Gena thought to herself, "Shawn is a very powerful man so whatever he's into it's too late to get out."

"You see Gena; I just wanna live an average life. I don't want people looking at me like I'm some kind'uv big shot. And that's why I go to work every day, so people can look at me as an average man and nothing more!"

"I see what you're saying honey. Look, I know it's our honeymoon, but how bout us leaving a little early going home. I'm enjoying myself and everything, but I'm on my period now, and I know you know how women act when they're on their period."

"Yes I do Mrs. Bomoski. We'll leave first thing tomorrow. I'll call Mack tonight to let'em know."

After they were done eating, Shawn left a hundred dollar tip on the table.

Gena smiled and said, "that was really delicious, I enjoyed every bite of that steak. We have to come back here soon someday Mr. Bomoski."

"Whenever you like honey, after all this is our restaurant too. What's mine is yours too. When Antonio gets grown, all of this power I have I'm goin give it to him. I needed a son in my life, and now that I have one, I'll treat'em like he was my very own, you'll see."

April 3, 1973

On the following day Gena and Shawn sat around the motel waiting for Mack to arrive at the airport.

Shawn said, "I know Mack got my message last night baby. He'll be here, but he's probably cussing us out all the way here. He just have to be mad, after all, I pay'em enough money to move his ass when I say move it. I just hope he went home last night and checked his answering machine."

Gena said, "he probably got the message. If he didn't we can't blame him; he thinks were going to be here till the fifth."

"Yeah your right. Well I guess I'll call Captain Redge while I'm still here."

Shawn dialed the number, the phone ringed four times. "Captain Redge speaking?"

"Bomoski, Captain."

"Before you say anything, everything is taken care of. Everything should go as planned, unless you can't catch up with your man's?"

"Oh don't worry, that sneaky ass bastard goin be around when I get back home. You know yourself that he goin try and hang around long as he can trying to find out whatever he can about me, and right now, he already know too much. When this is over I'll send you a nice, fat bonus. Do take care Captain, I'm out've here."

Shawn held the phone in his hand asking, "Gena would you like me to call the house?"

"No.... let's surprise them. I miss my baby and Paula. Shawn, can I ask you something while we're alone?"

"Sure baby, what is it?"

"Would it be okay for Paula to stay with us until she get on her feet. I told'er I had to talk with you first!"

"Why not, she can stay as long as you want'er too. It's all up to you baby."

"Thank you, I'll let'er know as soon as we get back. She's my best friend."

"Yes I know, I been around you two long enough to know that you two are best friends. I think you'll be a good influence on her. She needs somebody like you in her life. You're a very strong-minded woman. I got something for us to do while we wait on Mack. Why don't we listen to this," Shawn pulled out the video tape.

"Ooo Shawn, you didn't tell me Richard Pryor gave you a tape."

"I wanted to surprise you, now put it right there, "she kissed him.

"Well I'm surprised, now put it on. I'm ready to do some laughing."

"Yeah me too, oh Rich, that's my boy. I believe he can make it to the top if he leave that stuff alone!"

"You're kidding Shawn, you mean to tell me Richard Pryor is on dope?!"

"Unfortunately yeah."

"That's terrible, he'll learn one day. Well, while we're waiting on Mack to get here, I'm fix'n to take me a quick bath."

"Mind if I join you?"

"That depends on if you like your water candy apple red or not."

"Damn baby, I forgot you and Mother Nature had a thing going on."

"You don't have to remind me Shawn, I think it speaks for itself."

"I'm sorry baby, didn't mean to upset you."

"I wish you men could go through this experience just one time in your life, and see how y'all feel."

"I said I was sorry Gena."

"I'll forgive you this time."

While Gena went to take her bath, Shawn called Mack again. This time the answering machine didn't come on. "Good, he got my message. The answering machine is off, everything should be right on schedule."

Fifteen minutes later Gena came out the bathroom and got dressed, saying, "Shawn, I'm ready when you are."

"Let's ride, Mack should be here by now. We can grab a bite to eat after I turn the car in."

"Don't let me forget to get Paula a souvenir. I don't want her to think I totally forgot about'er. "

After they ate, they walked from gift shop to gift shop buying gifts.

Gena said, "ooh Shawn, I know she'll like this," Gena picked up a doll.

Shawn laughed. "A stuff baby doll? Come on Gena, you can do better than that for a best friend. How bout those gold mugs, she'll like this."

"Yeah those are beautiful; I'll get two of them, one for Leonard too."

Shawn thought to himself, "Leonard ain't goin need nothing where he's going. Maybe a cold glass of water because hell is where I'm goin send his ass. It's a shame you can't invite people over to your house without them moping around in your business. It's a shame he has to learn the hard way."

"See there you go again Shawn, in another one of your trances."

"I'm sorry baby, we better be going. Mack should be here by now. Let me pay for this stuff so we can get going."

Meanwhile, back at the house, Leonard had taken pictures of everything in Shawn's private room, took the films to Western Union, and phoned his partner at the Homicide and Narcotics Division.

Detective Sam answers the phone, "Homicide and Narcotics Divison, Detective Sam speaking."

"Look here Sam, this Leonard, I can't talk long. Listen to me, I have some films in your name at Western Union. I want you to pick them up today and have them developed."

"What's going on Leonard?"

"I'm on to something. I'll explain it to you later, just do what I ask you to do."

"All right man, damn, you ain't got'ah go off on me."

"I'm sorry man. I didn't mean to snap at you. Hey I got'ah go, talk to you later."

"Damn nigga hung up in my face. I wonder what he up to now? What the hell, I'll find out later."

Back in Vegas, Mack arrived and looked at his watch saying to himself, "now where in the hell could they be?"

Gena stepped out the airport and spotted Mack, and yelled out. "We're over here, we're on our way, let me get Shawn."

Gena went back inside and got Shawn saying, "honey, Mack is here."

"Well it's about time."

When they got to the jet Mack smiled. "Why hello you two love birds, sorry it took me so long. I got home a little late last night. I wasn't expecting you two till the fifth. Y'all just climb aboard and I'll have y'all home in no time."

April 4, 1973, 10:00 AM

After hours of flying, they were finally back in Detroit.

Shawn woke Gena up saying, "wake up baby, we're landing."

Gena yarned saying, "oh thank God, home sweet home."

Mack said, "well y'all, we're finally here. Why don't you two let me drive y'all home. It's the least I can do for being so late picking y'all up."

Shawn said, "Mack, my friendly pilot that sounds good to me."

After forty minutes of driving, they were finally home. "Why don't you come in and have a drink with me Mack?" Shawn asked lifting the luggage.

"I guess I can do that, after all I am on the ground now. I don't have to land my car, it's already landed. Besides, if I get to drunk I can always lay my head on one of your pillows."

"You sure can Mack. You're always welcome in our home. Ain't that right Gena?"

"That's right now will you come onnn."

Gena opened the door; Paula and Leonard were upstairs watching television. Gena yelled out loud, "we're back…."

Paula jumped out of the bed, Leonard right behind her. Paula ran straight to Gena and said, "oh girl it's good to see you. Y'all back kind'ah early ain't you?"

"Yeah, Shawn was goin call, but I said let's surprise them. I got you a souvenir."

"Where it's at girl?"

"It's inside the luggage. I'll get it in a minute. Hi Leonard, I got you something too."

"Thank you Gena! How was your honeymoon?" He asked smiling.

"I'll tell you guys all about it, but first let me go see my lil-man. I had a ball though. Where is he Paula?"

"He's upstairs sleep."

"Let me go wake'em up."

"Who are these two honeymooners Shawn?" Mack asked smiling.

"I'm sorry, Mack this is Paula and Leonard, everybody this is Mack."

"Leonard and Paula said at the same time, "nice to meet you Mack."

"Nice to meet you both."

"What will it be Mack, Scotch or Gin?" Shawn asked.

"Scotch on the rocks will be fine with me son."

"How bout you Leonard, would you like a drink?" Shawn asked.

"No thanks Shawn, I'll stick with the beer," he said smiling.

Paula smiled saying, "I'm going upstairs to help Gena unpack."

When Paula got to Gena she walked straight up to her and stuck her tongue in Gena's mouth, kissing her, and saying, "damn, I missed you. I wish nobody was here; I'd suck you up and down."

"Me too, but even if they weren't here I couldn't do nothing no'way."

"You don't have to say another word girl, I know what time it is."
Gena picked the baby up and said, "come on let's go join the rest of the gang."

Gena and Paula kissed again. "I know Leonard been wearing that thang out."

Paula laughed, "girl be for real; he hardly even looks at me. I believe he likes men." They both laughed as they headed downstairs.

"You think he really like men?"

"He sure don't act like he like he."

"Girl you are sick," Gena laughed.

"Not as sick as him; I know I got some good stuff girl."

"I can vote you on that one, you sure do, "she said laughing.

They all sat around in the living room reminiscing, laughing and joking about their childhood until Mack had enough to drink.

Mack said, "well Shawn, it's been nice chit-chatting with you guys, but it's time for me to be moving along."

Shawn said, "well I enjoyed your company. Do drop back by and see us again. By the way, I'm giving a little picnic at the island on the seventh, please feel free to drop by."

"Ah picnic," Gena said.

"Yes my love, a picnic. We've been having some pretty descent weather lately. I think a picnic would be nice, don't you Leonard?"

"Yeah man, that do sound good."

"Mack, just be there around three."

"I'll be there, see you guys later."

After Mack left, Shawn was sounding like he had a buzz as he said, "oh yeah Gena, did you talk to Paula about what we talked about back in Vegas? I think now would be a good time don't you Paula?"

Gena said, "I think you had too much to drink."

"I'll ask'er if you don't want too."

"Paula, Shawn agreed to let you stay here with us."

Leonard shook his head, saying, "yeahhh that hard stuff will do it every time, that's why I don't mess with it."

Gena yarned, "well you guys, I'm going upstairs and take me'ah nap. I sure hope this baby don't wake up before I do, \" Gena yarned again.

Paula said, "you goin get you some rest girl. If he wakes up I'll get'em."

"Thanks Paula, you're a life-saver."

"Remember Gena, that's what friends are for," she said smiling.

"I'll see you when I wake up."

Shawn had fallen asleep on the couch. Paula said, "you ain't goin take your husband with you?"

"Y'all let'em sleep. See you Leonard."

Gena was laughing going up the stairs and Paula said, "I know what you're laughing about girl. You aint right."

"What she laughing about?" Leonard asked sipping on his beer.

"You really don't wanna know; it's a woman thang."

"Yeahhh I bet it is. I'm going to lay down myself, I'm tired."

Two hours had passed, Paula and Shawn was the only twp woke. She could hear Shawn messing around in the kitchen by the sound of the dishes being moved around.

Paula said to herself, "I see Shawn is up, I better go check on'em."

When she got downstairs she found Shawn in the kitchen drinking coffee and said, "I thought that was you down are. Are you feeling okay?"

"I must've drunk too much. I'm okay though, where's everybody?"

"Everybody sleep," she said walking over to the cabinet to get a cup.

Shawn's eyes were glued to her ass as he thought to himself, "boy, I bet she got some good pussy. I should crack on'er for some."

Paula turned and briefly stared at Shawn and said, "what are you thinking about Shawn?"

"You really wanna know?"

"Yeah, I really wanna know."

"Well if you really wanna know, I was thinking I ain't never slept with a black woman before!"

"Well Shawn, perhaps if you play your cards right, maybe one day that might change. But it's hard for me to believe a man your class ain't never been with a black woman before. I got'ah tell you something; like the old saying goes, once you had black, you never go back. Trust me on that one. Tell me the truth you wanna sleep with me don't you? I can see it in your eyes; I can even see it in the print of your pants. Just talking to me makes your dick hard don't it? Man if you had a shot of some of this stuff you'll probably put in for a divorce!"

"I would give you anything you want if you slept with me just one time. One time is all I ask!"

"What about Gena?"

"She'll never know!"

"We'll work something out one day, just have patience," she said smiling.

"I want you now!"

"Now is not the right time; don't worry you'll get your chance one day."

"Can I just hold you in my arms one time?"

Paula walked over to him and sat on his lap moving her ass nice and slow in a circular motion. Shawn grabbed her ass and said, "damn I got to have you!"

They could hear somebody coming down the stairs. Paula quickly jumped up hopping to the nearest chair.

They quickly changed the subject as Gena walked in the kitchen asking, "how long you two been up?"

"Not long," Shawn answered. "We were just having a cup of coffee. Why don't you join us."

"I would love too. You would not believe the dream I had."

Shawn sipped his coffee and said, "why don't you tell us about it."

"I dreamed Leonard died. We all were at his funeral. I took a big keg of Coors' beer and poured it in his grave. Then I said," this all to hold you till you get to heaven. Then I woke up, now don't y'all say nothing to him about that dream."

Paula laughed the said, "don't worry girl, I wouldn't want nobody coming up to me telling me I dreamed you died. My lips are sealed."

"So are mines," Shawn said and then thought to himself. "Now that's one dream going to come true."

Paula smiled saying, "I better go check on'em. I hope he's still living Gena."

"Don't go waking him up Paula. It was just'ah dream, my goddd."

"I want girl, and besides I got'ah go check on lil-man anyway."

"So Shawn, how you feeling?" Gena asked, pouring her coffee.

"My head is still spinning. Other than that I'm fine."

"You should'nah drink so much."

"I only had'ah few baby."

"Ah few all right; more like the whole bottle. You and Mack drunk a whole bottle of Scotch by y'all selves."

"Damn, no wonder my head feel like it's on cloud nine."

The phone started ringing; Gena answered it, "hello."

"Yes, is Bomoski in?"

"Yes, just'ah minute." Gena handed the phone over to Shawn.

"Shawn speaking."

"Hello Shawn."

"Sorcerer, now what'ah surprise. It's been'ah long time."

"Cut the talk Bomoski, I heard about the little problem. You make sure it's taken care of. I don't need your government breathing down my back. We have been doing to good for some punk ass detective to come along and fuck things up. Take care of it! If you need me you know where I'm at. By the way, that package you ordered will be there as scheduled!"

"Don't worry Sorcerer, I have everything under control."

"Good-day Bomoski."

After Shawn hung the phone up, Gena asked, "who was that? I know that voice from somewhere."

"That was just'ah old friend, nobody special."

"I know that voice; it'll come to me later," she said to herself.

April 6, 1973

Three days later, the two hit-men arrived in Detroit at 3:30P.M. as planned. Both men were dressed in an all black two-piece suit. They took a cab to the Millender Center, where Shawn sat patiently in his office waiting their arrival.

When they got to the front desk the tallest of the two men did all the talking since his English was much plainer.

"We like to see Shawn Bomoski. Could you direct us to him pleazzzz."

"Sure," the secretary said smiling. "He's on the tenth floor. You can take the elevator, they're right behind you."

"Thank you much."

The hit-men knocked on the door. "Come in please," Shawn said.

As they entered the room, Shawn said, "gentlemen, welcome to Detroit. I don't have to tell y'all what your mission is."

The hit-men didn't say a word as they focused on what Shawn had to say. "Tomorrow around this time, you two will be dressed as detectives. I have a plain car waiting for y'all in the parking lot. Y'all will find a change of clothes and in the pants pocket you'll find your badges. In the glove-compartment y'all will find the guns. Nine-millimeter should get the job done. You see this tape right here, I want him to hear it before he dies."

The hit-men took the tape out of Shawn's hand and bowed. Shawn said, "one more thing; y'all will have cell-phones in the car. Before y'all kill'em I wanna hear his voice. My number will be on the phone and the directions to where he will be. Y'all be there at three and no later than three!"

"We will be there!"

"Hear this good; make sure he hears the tape before y'all call me. Here's a little bonus for now, its fifty bands. Enjoy y'all selves; I'll see you two tomorrow."

Both men bowed their heads to Shawn and left the office, and as soon as they left Shawn called home.

"Hello, Bomoski resident Paula speaking."

"Hey Paula, this Shawn."

"Oh, hi Shawn."

"Where's my wife?"

"Leonard took her to the store to pick up a few things for the baby."

"So her and Leonard went shopping together?"

"Yes, her and Leonard, you know she don't have'ah car."

"How long they been gone?"

"I'll say about five minutes, you just…missed her."

"I'll be home shortly, see you when I get there, bye."

"Bye Shawn," she said hanging up.

Shawn rushed out his office talking to himself. "Man I hope I get home before Gena gets back."

Shawn hopped on the freeway doing forty over the speed limit. Thirty minutes later he was pulling in the driveway saying to himself, "I don't see Leonard car nowhere."

Shawn rushed in the house. Paula was sitting in the living-room watching television. Her eyes got wide when she saw that it was Shawn coming through the living-room front door. She said, "damn, you got here quick. Where were you across the street?"

"Actually I was trying to beat Gena and your boy Leonard here."

"Well you have certainly done that now what's up with you?"

"You already know how bad I want you Paula!"

Paula walked up to Shawn and rubbed her hands gently across his face asking, "how bad do you want me Mr. Bomoski?"
"I'll give you anything you want just make love with me!"

"How bout making a check out for let's say, ten-thousand!"

"You got it, I'll write it out right now. Now please, before somebody come, show me what you got."

Paula took the gum she was chewing out of her mouth and dropped it on the floor and said, "get on your knees and pick it up with your mouth."

Shawn got on both knees and picked the gum up with his mouth. Paula pulled down her panties to her knees while she watched him come up with the gum in his mouth.

"How does it taste?" She asked.

"Sweet," he said as his eyes stared at the black hairs on Paula's cunt.

Paula took her finger and pointed it down at her cherry saying, "not as sweet as this I'm fix'n to give you."

Paula dropped to her knees and unzipped Shawn's pants, pulling them down to his knees. His cock rose immediately as Paula put her mouth on his soldier, saying, "I want you to stick this dick right here." She spread her legs wide open while he drove his cucumber inside her sizzling hot cherry.

Paula moaned in passion as she ran her hands up and down Shawn's back saying, "damn Shawn… you feel good."

"Not bad for a white-boy huh?"

Paula moaned, "not bad at all."

130

"Damn you got some good pussy. I'm about to come; I ain't never came this quick, Ahhh, ahhh, yesss."

"Yes Shawn, yes, cumm in this pussy."

Shawn unloaded his load. Paula pushed him to the side and put her clothes on.

Shawn said, "Damn that was good. You got let me get it again."

"I don't think so. You got what you wanted, now give me my check!"

"I don't know what you got in that pussy. I mean, ain't no woman never made me come that quick."

"Not even Gena?"

"Not even Gena," he said passing her the check for ten-thousand.

Paula thought to herself as she took the check out his hand. "Damn, this the quickest ten-thousand dollars I ever made and I didn't even buss'ah nut. It's goin cost twice as much if he gets some more of this stuff. He do have a nice size penis for a white boy. He just can't handle this between my legs.

Shawn sat back in the love-seat thinking to himself, "I got to hit that ass again. I know one thing for sure now; she do got some good sex."

Twenty-minutes later, Gena and Leonard walked through the door, each holding shopping bags in their hands.

"Hi Shawn, "Gena said. "I had to pick-up a few things for the picnic tomorrow."

Shawn said, "silly me, I should've known what you went to do when Paula said you went shopping for the baby. I hope you bought plenty to drink."

"Yes I did. Leonard you can put those bags in the kitchen for me if you don't mind."

"What's up Shawn?" Leonard asked.

"Nothing much, how's everything with you? How you feeling today?"

"I guess I'll make it. I'll feel even better once I sit these heavy bags in the kitchen. Gena bought cases of beer, I can't wait till tomorrow."

"Neither can I," Shawn said.

Leonard took the bags in the kitchen and came right back, saying, "mannn, we have enough beer to get'ah army drunk. Speaking of army Shawn, have you ever been in?"

"Nope, why do you ask? Do I look like the army type?"

"Not really."

Leonard was hoping he said, "yes" to the question. That might of explained all the weapons he possessed.

Shawn thought to himself, "yeahhh this motha-fucka is really trying to find out about me. His questioning days will be over tomorrow. Let me ask you a question Leonard?"

"Go right ahead."

"How long have you been in your line of work?"

"As a matter, next month will be eighteen years for me."

"And what is it that you do again?"

"I'm in the landscaping business. I have a crew that I work with."

Shan thought to himself, "this punk actually thinks I believe this shit. That's why I boned your woman. I'll tell'em before I kill'em. Damn, I completely forgot about Mo, let me call'em up. Excuse me for a minute Leonard, I got to make a quick phone call."

Shawn dialed the number. The secretary answered, "this is Mr. Bomoski, put Mo on the phone please."

"Right away Mr. Bomoski."

Seconds later, "Mo speaking."

"Hello Mo."

"Shawn my man, when did you get back?"

"I been back a couple of days now and sorry I'm just now calling. How's everything going there? No more dead bodies I hope!"

"No, no more dying. Everything's going great so far."

"That's good; what I really called you for is to see if you'd like to join me tomorrow at the island for a little picnic we're giving?"

"I'd love too, what time?"

"We'll be there around two-thirty."

"I'll see you there."

"Good, I'll see you tomorrow then. Tell everyone back there I said hello, good bye."

"Later man."

Shawn said to himself after he hung the phone up, "I hope Gena don't ask me who I was on the phone talking too. Every time I get on the phone she wanna know who I'm talking too." He walked by her. "Good, she didn't ask this time. She should be off her period by now. It's been a few days now, I guess I'll screw her tonight, she got some good stuff too."

Twenty minutes later, Gena had finally got supper ready and said to Paula, "Paula darling, call in the living room and tell them dinner's ready."

Paula shouted, "dinner ready, y'all better come and get it."

Gena fixed Shawn and her plate. She sat down and started eating before Leonard and Shawn got in the kitchen.

Paula got up and fixed a plate for her and Leonard.

When Shawn walked in the kitchen he said, "damn, this food smells delicious."

Leonard walked in a few minutes after Shawn. Gena's eyes were glued to the print in Leonard's pants as she said to herself, "boyyy, Leonard sure do have a big cock. I don't think I could handle all that man in me. Paula, I feel sorry for you, black men do have some big cocks. I remember when "Tee" use to bang me; he had a big cock. I think I'll stick with my Shawn, he has enough for me. I think I'll surprise him tonight when I walk in the bedroom wearing my red silk negligee that he bought me for Christmas."

After dinner they all sat around in the living room watching television.

Gena said, "let me go check on my son."

Paula said, "I'll go with you, I don't like this show anyway."

When they got upstairs Gena reached in the baby's crib. She picked him and put him back down, then turned to Paula and said, "give me a kiss."

After they were tongue kissing, Paula pulled away saying, "we better stop before somebody catches us."

"Just hold me for a few more seconds, and then we can go." Paula held her. "Damn, your body feels so good next to mine's, okay he can go now."

When they got back downstairs Shaw said, "what took y'all so long? Y'all missing the movie."

"I had to show Gena how to put'ah diaper on," Paula said laughing. "I'm just kidding, we were playing with the baby." She looked over at the baby. "Look at'em, he's so cute, remind me of my son when he was that size."

Gena said, "speaking of your son, I would like to see them pretty hazel brown eyes. Why don't we call your mom and see about picking him up. He can go to the picnic with us tomorrow."

"That do sound good. I'll call her now and let'er know."
Paula made the call and Sharon answered, "hello."

"Hi mama what you doing?"

"Hi baby, I was just thinking about you a few minutes ago."

"Oh yeah, mama, I was thinking about picking my son up tonight if it's okay with you."

"If it's okay with me? Hell yeahhh its okay with me, I need'ah break."

"Thanks mama, we having a picnic tomorrow. I'll talk to you when I get out there."

"Okay, see you when you get here."

"I'm on my way, bye mama."

Paula got off the phone smiling. Gena asked, "well what did she say?"

"She said I could come get him."

"Well let's go, I'll wrap the baby up real good and take him with us. Leonard, you can stay and keep Shawn company; we shouldn't be that long."

Shawn said, "you guys can take my car. I got a full tank of gas, that way y'all want have to stop for nothing unless y'all want too."

"Be back in a few Leonard," Paula said heading out the door.

"Okay baby, drive careful."

Forty-minutes later they were knocking on Sharon's door. Normally Paula had her own key, but things had changed.

After a few knocks they could hear Sharon saying, "who is it?"

"It's me mama, your one and only daughter."

Sharon opened the door and smiled saying," look at you, my God, you are so healthy looking. Y'all come on in here."

Paula and Sharon hugged. Tears ran down both their face as they embraced.

"Mama this is my best friend, Gena this is my mama."

"Nice to meet you Gena. You can call me mama too and who is this lil-angel?" Sharon asked smiling.

"This lil-angel is my son. His name is Antonio," Gena said smiling.

"Hey there lil-fella, he's so cute. Paula, I know you bought me something to drink with you?"

"No mama I didn't. I thought you stop drinking, but I see you haven't."

"Girl who paying you to think? Now give your mama a few dollars, I'll find somebody to take me to the store."

"Just chill-out mama, where's my son?"

"I got'em dressed. He fell asleep waiting on you to get here. I already packed his things, now come on girl. Let's catch the liquor store before they close."

"I see you still love to drink."

"Hay, you do your thang and let me do mines, okay. What you say your name was again baby?"

"Gena."

"Gena, take mama to the liquor store before they close okay. Damn, what Paula talking about."

"Where's the store mama?"

"Right down the street, come baby, let's hurry."

"Come on mama, I'll run you to the store," Gena said smiling.

Paula just looked at her mama and smiled saying, "You're a trip mama."

"N'all you the trip. We'll be right back, you just watch the kids. Can you do that for me?"

When Sharon and Gena got in the car Sharon said, "you got any money baby, I wanna get me a pint, but I'm a little short."

"How much is the pint mama?"

"Twelve dollars."

"I tell you what mama, you just hold on to your money. I'm goin buy you a fifth of whatever you drink."

"Cognac baby, mama drink the best. I really appreciate it baby. I just spent my whole check on that boy. Mama don't have no money; my checks don't be bout shit!"

"Well mama, tonight I'm buying the drink, plus I'm goin give you a hundred dollars to put in your pockets."

"Lord, I hope this store ain't closed. I see some cars, it's not closed yet, hurry baby, mama ain't had'ah drink all day. I know what you thinking baby, you saying to yourself she's an alcoholic. No, no baby I ain't no alcoholic. Ah alcoholic drink anything you put in front of him. Mama only drinks Martel; that's Cognac, nothing, but the best."

Gena laughed, "I never thought that about you mama, I think you're a good woman. Any woman who can take care of someone else's child is a good woman in my book and for that alone you deserve a drink!"

Sharon stayed in the car while Gena went in the store. Sharon was five-foot-six, chocolate complexion, pretty dark brown eyes, and well put together for a woman in her early forties.

"Here you go mama, all for you, and I didn't forget your cigarettes," she said handing Sharon the bag.

"Thank you baby, you know the way back don't you?"

"Yes, straight ahead."

When they got back to Sharon's house, Paula opened the door saying, "mama your refrigerator is ridiculous. Where's the food?"

"Girl, I got my food stamps, but I ain't got nobody to take me grocery shopping yet." Sharon poured herself a drink. "Don't worry bout what's in this one, we eat everyday in this house."

Paula whispered in Gena's ear saying, "come on girl, we better get going cause once she take that first sip she goin me and you out in about a minute after. I know'er like a book." Paula looked at her mama. "Mama we bout to leave, I'll bring'em home in a few days, I love you!"

"Yeahhh right, I love you too."

"Mama don't drink all that liquor tonight okay!"

"Gena baby, get this nut out my house. Don't drink all the liquor, you got your nerves."

Gena smiled, "see, I told you girl she got Mr. Cognac in her system now. She don't want to hear nothing we got to say, let's ride. Come on lock the door behind me mama."

"Go head on Paula, mama got it. I ain't drunk, not yet."

When they got in the car both babies were still sleep. Paula said, "girl, I hope this boy don't wake up tripping. He don't even know who I am!"

"Don't worry, your his mother, and believe me he knows his mother."

"I hope your right honey."

"Trust me Paula, he know you are, now quit worrying."

Forty-five minutes later, Leonard was still sitting in the living room watching television when Paula and Gena walked in the house holding the babies in their arms.

"Where's Shawn?" Gena asked.

"He just went upstairs about ten minutes ago."

"Well that's where I'm going too, good night you two."

When Gena got to the bedroom Shawn was laying down in the bed gazing at the ceiling. Gena smiled and said, "you can just get on up from there, I have a treat for you tonight."

I can't wait," Shawn said smiling.

"I'll be right back, let me lay him down, don't you go nowhere."

"I'll be right here."

Gena came back in the bedroom wearing her red silk negligee. Shawn's eyes were glued on her as he watched her walk towards the bed. Shawn said, "baby you sure do look sexy as hell in that negligee."

"Whyyy thank you darling and everything under this red sexy negligee is yours to do what you wish."

Gena got on top of Shawn and rode him like she was riding a Mustang. Every sound and motion Gena made Shawn thought about Paula and when he pictured Paula on top of him he began to come. They made love for about an hour before they both fell asleep in each other's arms.

A cry in the middle of the night woke Gena up and she could hear Paula's voice and said to herself, "well Paula has everything under control, let me get some sleep. I see Shawn's ass is knocked out, I wish I could sleep that good."

April 7, 1973

The next day Paula was the first one up. She peaked in at the kids and saw that they were still sleep so she went downstairs and put on a pot of coffee and started making breakfast saying to herself, "I guess I can scramble ah egg and fry ah sausage."

It wasn't long before everyone in the house was up. Gena had Stan with her and said to him, "come on son, your mommy is in the kitchen." Entering the kitchen, "Paula, somebody wanna see you."

"I'm in the kitchen," Paula called out. "And all who are hungry better come and get it."

Gena smiled, "there's your mommy."

Stan ran straight to Paula. She picked him up and kissed him on the lips saying, "come on eat some breakfast for mommy, you hungry?"

"Unnn huh," Stan answered.

Paula spread some newspaper in the middle of the floor for Stan and said, "Gena, girl you was right. He do know who his mama is. I'm so he's with me, I even feel like a mother again. What's my name Stan? Say ma-ma," Stan looked at her and smiled. "Say ma-ma."

"Ma-ma," he said smiling.

Paula laughed and said, "just to hear you say that makes my day son!"

Gena smiled saying, "don't worry girl he'll be calling you mama so much you goin wish he couldn't talk."

"You think so."

"I know so, look at'em with his handsome self, and girl he do have some pretty eyes. I'll be so glad when Antonio learns how to talk. The first thing I'm goin teach'em is how to say mama."

Shawn smirked saying, "the first thing I'm goin teach'em is how to fish."

Gena smiled, "yeahhhh, you make sure you teach'em how to clean'em too," they all laughed.

Friday April 8, 1973 3:00 P.M.

Gena fried some chicken and made sandwiches for the picnic. Shawn and Leonard loaded everything in the back of Shawn's station-wagon while Paula got the kids dressed.

They arrived on the island at 2:45P.M., and stopped at the first available picnic table.

As Shawn parked, Mo pulled up right behind him. Mo was the first to get out his car with his lady friend following. Lisa Mcdyce, was the five-foot-six, blue eyed, thirty-year old lady's name. She wore blue jeans and a red blouse to go along with her tan brown complexion.

Shawn and the crew got out the vehicle. Shawn said, "what's up Mo, glad you could make it, I see you brought'ah friend."

"Yeahhh man, this is Lisa, Lisa I would like you to meet my best friend Shawn, and this is his lovely wife Gena."

"Nice to meet you Lisa," Gena said.

Mo said," this is Paula, I don't know my man here."

"Oh I'm sorry Mo," Shawn said. "This is Leonard, Paula's boyfriend."

"Please to meet you Leonard," Mo said shaking his hand.

"Pleased to meet you too Mo!"

Gena smiled saying, "well since we all know each other now, let's set the table and enjoy the picnic."

Shawn grabbed the cooler saying, "I agree anybody for an ice cold beer or a hot cup of tea if you know what I mean?"

"I most certainly do, but I think I'll stick with the ice cold beer."

"Help yourselves," Shawn said out loud. "The cooler is right here."

They sat around the picnic table drinking beer after beer, chit-chatting about how nice the weather had been lately.

Shawn chugged another beer down and said, "we sure have had some good damn weather here lately."

"We sure have," Lisa said smiling.

Paula laughed saying, "let's not brag on it too much. Y'all know how the weather here in Detroit is; it's subject to snow tonight so let's enjoy this little break while we can."

Gena said, "Shawn darling, I'm so glad you picked today to come out for a breath of fresh air."

"Not as glad as I am," Shawn said looking at his watch, saying to himself, "damn its one minute to three. They should have been here by now. Bingo, here they come now, right on time."

The two hit-men got out the unmarked car dressed like detectives with their badges to their sides noticeable enough to know that they were the law."

As they approached the picnic table, one stood back while the other one talked. "Sir, is your name Leonard Boston?"

"Yes, I'm Leonard Boston, what can I do for you?"

"Mr. Boston, we have a warrant for your arrest. Now would you peacefully come with us please?"

"Wait'ah minute, this must be some kind of mistake. I ain't never been in no kind'uv trouble with the law before."

Everybody at the picnic table stared at Leonard not believing what was going on and was curious to know, till they heard the detectives saying, "sir the charge not that serious. I'm sure you heard of Friend of Court."

Leonard's mind was at ease as he said, "Friend of Court, officer I don't even have'ah kid. This got to be some kind of mistake."

"Well sir, if it mistake, you have nothing to worry about. You'll be returning to friends in no time, but right now you must come with us!"

"I'm coming, I guess I don't have much of a choice. You're not going to hand-cuff me are you?"

"No need, charge not serious."

"Shawn, Paula, you guys excuse me, this shouldn't take long."

Shawn stood up saying, "if you need me Leonard, you know where I'm at!"

"Thanks Shawn, but I won't be needing any help. I'll be back before you can drink three more beers."

Mo said, "he'll be back shortly especially if he don't have any kids."

The unmarked car pulled off, Shawn quietly sat in the backseat, and after they were out of Shawn's sight, Leonard said, "let me explain something to y'all before we go through all this unnecessary bullshit. If one of y'all would take a look at my identification, y'all will see that I'm a private detective."

The hit-man on the passenger side turned around saying, "yeah, we know who you are Mr. Boston and that's why we here!"

The driver pulled into a dead-end street as Leonard said, "what you mean that's why you here?"

"Shut the fuck up, you die today motha-fucka!" The passenger said as he pointed the gun.

Leonard stared at the barrel of the nine millimeter and said, "what's going on? What's with the gun?!"

The driver said," I have something for you to hear before we kill you." He reached in his coat pocket and pulled the tape out. "This tape made especially for you." He pushed the tape in, Shawn started talking… "You recognize my voice private detective?"

"Yeah it's Shawn."

Leonard listened closely as Shawn's voice said," what's up Leonard, I guess you're wondering what's going on. I'll start by saying you fucked with the wrong man this time. Don't nobody fuck around in my private affairs. Today you goin wish you was a landscaper. Be seeing you in hell. Oh by the way, Paula do have some good pussy. Take care y'all business fellaz, call me right now!"

The passenger dialed the number and put Leonard on the cell phone. Shawn said, "hello Leonard, we miss you here."

"Please Shawn, don't this to me man, I'll stay away. I don't know anything. Please Shawn!"

"Yeahhh just what I wanted to hear, you begging like'ah bitch. Sorry Leonard you already know too much. This will teach you not to screw around with me and by the way, I enjoyed every moment with your girlfriend!"

"Whyyyy you dirty son-of-a-bitch."

"Goodbye Leonard."

"Wait'ah minute man."

The passenger snatched the phone out Leonard's hand while the driver shot Leonard three times in the head. Shawn could hear gun shots as the passenger said to him," Bomoski our job is done, we go now!"

149

"Well done, y'all will receive y'all pay when y'all return to Columbia. Pleasure doing business with you!"

Shawn turned the cell-phone off and joined the rest of his guests. Meanwhile, back at the unmarked police car, the driver leaned over the seat to make sure the job was completed and unknowingly dropped the tape Shawn recorded out his picket. "He's dead, let's get out of here, and go to the airport now."

Back at the picnic Paula was saying, "damn Leonard been gone a long time. I'll call down to the precinct when we get home. We better get going; it looks like it's about to rain."

Gena said, "it does look cloudy. I'll grab the kids. What time is it Shawn? "

"It's going on eight honey."

"You can grab the cooler and Mo you can take some of that beer with you if you like," Gena said.

"I'll do just that Gena."

One hour later they were home at last. Paula went straight to the telephone. Gena said, "Girl who you calling?"

"I'm calling downtown to the police station. Leonard's car is here. I wanna find out where he at so I can at least take his car so he can a ride when he get out of there."

"Yes, 13th Precinct, Sgt, Brute speaking."

"Yes, I'm calling to see if you was holding a Leonard Boston. He was picked up today for child support."

"Hold on ma'am I'll go see." A few minutes go by. "No ma'am, no Leonard Boston is here, maybe they let'em go."

"Thank you very much sir." Paula hung up and said to herself, "o'well, he know where I live, and he know where his car at. He'll catch up with me when he gets out."

Three hours later, Shawn, Gena, and Paula sat around in the living room watching television. Paula was on her way to bed until she heard the eleven o'clock news reporter say, "this is Bill Bonds, channel seven action news. Our top story tonight; a black male was found shot three times in the head on the eastside of Detroit. Police investigators describe the man to be in his early thirties, to be one of their own. The I.D. card found in the man's pocket definitely is from a detective known as Leonard A. Boston."

Paula cried out, "God no, it can't be, this can't be true!"

Gena put her arms around Paula to comfort her. "It can't be true, he was just with us," Gena said as they continued to listen to the news.

"Police are saying this tragic was no accident; whoever killed the detective certainly was professional. So far there has been no clue or evidence in the unmarked squad car to link anyone to the murder. Detroit Police are doing a full investigation. I just got word that Chief of Police Berry Tuckers says that whoever did this to Leonard

151

Boston wasn't too professional or they wouldn't have left the tape with the killer's voice on it, and he's determined to find this killer."

Shawn couldn't believe his ears and thought to himself, "these stupid motha-fuckaz left the damn tape, now I really got'ah problem."

Bill Bond continues, "we are going live over to the Chief of Police. Chief Tucker do you think this killing was drug related?"

"Well it's hard to say right now what caused this killing. If I come up with anything you'll be the first to know. But I can tell you this much, the tape we have on evidence is the key to solving this case."

"Thank you Chief Tucker and good luck, this is Bill Bonds signing off of channel seven action news."

Shawn thought to himself, "I got to contact Sorcerer first thing in the morning. I don't know where he found those two careless sons-of-bitches. I can't believe they actually left the fuck'n tape. Shit, how stupid can you get?"

Paula and Gena embraced each other as Paula cried saying, "I had no idea he was a detective. Who would wanna kill a detective? Life is just too short Gena; one minute you're here and the next minute you're dead. He was so young."

Gena wiped the tears from Paula's eyes and said, "he sure had me fooled. I thought he was a landscaper for real. I guess when you're doing detective work its best not to tell nobody!"

"Yeah, I guess you're right. I'm going to lie down, I don't feel too good. I'll see you in the morning."

"Okay, you get some rest, I'm sorry about Leonard."

Shawn yarned saying, "I guess I'll turn in too, goodnight everybody."

Shawn laid in the bed thinking about all the trouble he was in, and how he was going to get out of it. "If Gena and Paula found out I had Leonard killed what would they think of me? Mannn I got myself in some deep shit, I got to be dreaming. This can't be happening to me; the police goin be on my ass in a matter of time, and maybe they want. I didn't put my last name on the tape, just my first. They won't have nothing, but a voice to work with, and that ain't enough, so they really don't have nothing on me. Let me go to sleep, I'm straight. I'll call Sorcerer in the morning and tell'em he sent me two fuck-ups, as a matter of fact get rid of their sorry ass. If they that carless they not professionals; I should have them took out."

Shawn leaned over on Gena's side of the bed and turned the radio on and slowly drifted off to sleep.

Gena talked Paula into staying up a little while longer with her downstairs. They ended up falling asleep on the sofa, while the kids slept silently through the night.

April 9, 1973 10:00 A.M.

Shawn was the first to wake up. Looking over to the other side of the bed, not seeing Gena, and said to himself, "maybe she's downstairs making breakfast."

When Shawn got downstairs he saw Gena and Paula curled up together on the living-room sofa, and said to himself, "damn, they sleeping like they husband and wife. I hope what I'm thinking ain't true. They act like they screwing or something. I guess when your best friends you can do things like that. O'well, let me go freshen up."

Before Shawn could reach the stairs the phone ringed. He ran upstairs to catch it in the bedroom, "hello."

"This Mo man; man did you see the news last night?"

"Yeah I did, shame isn't it?"

"Man they took that man out execution style. I couldn't believe it; all of us were just at the picnic together drinking beer. The news said he was some kind of investigator. He must'ah investigated the wrong person this time!"

"Well whatever he was into or doing don't matter now, he's dead. Look I was just on my way to the bathroom to freshen up; I'll get back with you later on today."

"That's cool, talk to you later."

"O'k Mo talk to you later. I hear the baby crying and Gena and Paula is still sleep."

After Mo hung up Shawn went to see about Antonio, and when he got to the baby he said, "what's wrong lil-fella? You got to quiet down, you will wake up Stan with all this fussing you doing here. Suck on this bottle for a minute. You don't know me very well right now, but one day you will. One day you goin be a powerful man; yeahhh that's right my son, I do mean powerful. You just suck on that bottle for now. Poppa will be back as soon as I get out the shower, okay."

After Shawn got out the shower he decided it was a good time to call Sorcerer. He put his jogging suit on and dialed the number. "Hello," the voice on the end said.

"This Bomoski let me speak with Sorcerer."

After a brief pause Sorcerer came to the phone. "Sorcerer speaking."

"We have a problem!"

"What do you mean we have a problem? Didn't my men take care of that for you?"

"Your men fucked up!"

"What you mean they fucked up?"

"I gave them a tape with me saying goodbye to this bastard and one of them careless bastards left the tape in the car where the shit took place!"

Sorcerer's voice turned into rage as he said, "you said my men fucked up, no I don't think so you stupid son-of-a-bitch, you fucked up! I sent my men to do a job and they did what they were paid to do and you, your dumb ass gave them a stupid ass tape to play. What kind of fool are you? Out of all my years in this business I ain't never seen a man in our type of business play a tape on the job. I can't believe you did that stupid shit. I tell you something else. I'm running a nationwide business, and if you put my life in jeopardy I'll have you killed before you can blink an eye. If my name be printed or mentioned in your so called America papers I'm coming for your careless ass. I hope I make myself clear!"

"Now wait'ah minute Sorcerer. I helped you build this business from the ground up, I have as much."

Sorcerer cut him off. "You have nothing, I run this shit, and ain't nobody I mean nobody goin put my life in jeopardy not even you. You just make sure my name stays clear down there and everything will remain the same with you and me. That is all I ask of you, now you have a nice day, and give my blessing to the misses, good day Bomoski!"

Shawn hung the phone up and checked on the kids. They both was woke so he took them downstairs with him and said, "oooo ladies, it's time to rise and shine, I brought you both some company."

Gena yarned and said, "boyyy I was sleeping my butt off, what time is it?"

"It's a quarter after eleven," Shawn answered. "I'm going out to do me some jogging, so you two might as well get on up from there."

Paula got on up saying, "you could have let me sleep a little while longer."

"No I couldn't, it's almost twelve o'clock."

Gena said, "well we're up now. You can go on and do what you are going to do."

"I'll see you guys in a few hours."
"Okay honey, would you turn the T.V. on for me on your way out?"

"What channel?"

"It don't matter."

Shawn turned the television station to channel fifty. Paula said, "oue leave it there, they'll probably be talking about Leonard in the morning news."

"I'm gone, it's too early for me to be hearing about the dead again."

Five minutes after Shawn walked out the door the phone ringed and Paula answered, "Hello Paula speaking?"

"Yes is Shawn in Paula this Mo."

"Nope, he just stepped out Mo. I believe he said he was going jogging."

"I'll catch'em later on, so how you feeling Paula?"

"I'm feeling okay."

"I'm sorry to hear bout your friend."

"So am I!"

"Look Paula, I know this isn't the right time, but I was wondering, would you like to catch a movie or something and a perhaps a dinner afterwards? What I'm trying to say is, I like you a lot, and I just might have something you'll enjoy. Please say you'll go out with me."

"I guess we can go on a date one time, but I'm goin tell you this one time and one time only, please don't try to give me any drugs. I'm not with that program anymore, and if you trick me like you tricked me before, I'll kill you!"

"Don't worry Paula, I want try anything like that."

"I'm serious Mo, I swear on my son's life, I will kill you!"

"So how does this weekend sound to you?"

"Good, I'll pick you up Friday. See you then, tell Shawn I called."

"Good day Mo."

Paula hung the phone up smiling. "Who was that Paula?" Gena asked.

"Oh girl that was Mo, he wanna take me out this Friday."

"I hope he don't."

Paula cut her off, "don't even worry girl, I already told him. Drugs is a no-no, I'm not going back to living that way again!"

"You be careful, I don't trust that man at all!"

"Don't worry Gena, I'm only going out with him to get out the house for a change of scenery, and plus, there's a movie I been wanting to see. Why don't you and Shawn join us?"

"No thanks girlfriend, this weekend Shawn and I are going to spend all our time in that bedroom upstairs if you know what I mean."

"You know I do girl."

Meanwhile, while Shawn was busy jogging, Leonard's partner, Detective Sam drove out to Sears' to get the pictures developed Leonard had sent to him. Sam was curious to see what on the pictures was so important to Leonard.

Sam pulled his car over to the side of the road to take a peek at the photos. The first picture he looked at was of the guns, and the next picture was of Sorcerer posing in his army fatigues.

Detective Sam said out loud, "I know this man, this is Sorcerer; Columbia's biggest drug dealer. Now I know why Leonard was killed; he was on to something, and Sorcerer is behind all of this. I'm goin get to the bottom of this if it's the last thing I do. Leonard was like a brother to me, he taught me everything I know about investigating. Don't worry Leonard somebody goin pay for your death. Since I'm out here I'll go pay your mother a visit."

Sam drove straight to Leonard's mother's house. Mrs. Boston was sitting on the front porch in her wooden rocking chair, and as soon as she saw Sam getting out the car, tears started running down her face.

"Hi Mrs. Boston," Leonard said.

"Hi baby, my Leonard was a good boy. He wouldn't hurt ah fly. They killed the only I had left in this world!"

"I know, Leonard was a good detective, he didn't deserve this!" He said putting his arm around her shoulder.

"You got to find the man who killed my son!"

"Yes ma'am I'll find'em. Leonard was like a brother to me, I miss him already!"
"The police said on the news last night they had a tape of the man's voice who murdered my son."

"I didn't know about the tape Mrs. Boston. I think I'm on to something. I best get back to the station, and don't worry Mrs. Boston, I'm goin catch that killer, that, I can promise you!"

"God bless you son."

Sam kissed her on the forehead saying, "I'll be back to see you again. If you need me for anything you know where you can reach me."

"All I want you to do for me is catch the man who killed my son!"

"I'll get'em, you have a nice day!"

Sam rushed back to the precinct to find out what was on the tape he knew nothing about.

When Sam got to the station he went straight to the evidence room. "Hi Terry, give me everything you got on the Leonard Boston killing."

"Give me a second," the officer said searching for his keys. "You been up north lately Sam?"

"N'all haven't had a chance, been too damn busy working."

"I heard that, hear you go, this is everything. Damn shame what happened to Leonard ain't it?"

"Yeah, I know, thanks Terry!"

"Anytime Sam!"

Detective Sam went straight to his office and played the tape he got from the evidence room. As he continued listened he said to himself, "I know that name from somewhere, Shawn, Shawn, Shawn. Bingo, I got it, Leonard asked me to run a check on Shawn somebody. Where's that paper, I wrote the name down somewhere."

Sam scrambled through the papers on his desk. "Yes, got it, Shawn Bomoski, this is the man responsible for killing Leonard. This son-of-a-bitch goin do some time in prison if I don't kill'em first. This turned out to be a good day after all."

Shawn phoned the house from the donut shop. Gena answered, "hello."

"Hi sweetheart, I'm at the donut shop having a cup of coffee, I'll be home in a few. How's everything at the house?"

"Fine, I thought you were out jogging?"

"I was, but I thought I would jog on down to the donut shop and grab a cup of coffee."

"Okay darling, I'll see you when you get here. Oh, if I'm not here when you get home I went with Paula to take the baby home."

"Okay baby, talk to you later."

Paula was standing behind Gena playing with Gena's ear while she talked on the phone, "stop it Paula."

"Who you talking to Gena?"

"That's Paula playing with me, with her crazy self."

"Well I'm gone."

"Bye honey," she said hanging up.

Back at the police station, Sam phoned the front desk. "This is Detective Sam; I would like to put out an A.P.B on a Leonard Boston case. I believe we have a suspect; pick up a Shawn Bomoski, and lieutenant I would like the media in on this one."

Within minutes Shawn Bomoski's name was being spoken on every television station in Detroit, along with a picture of him and Sorcerer posing together.

Shawn was still at the donut shop sipping on coffee, and watching the dating game on the thirteen inch television that sat across from him over the counter.

The program was interrupted. "We interrupt this program to bring you this special news update on the murder of a well respected detective. I'm Bill Bonds, channel seven actions news. Leonard Boston was murdered just yesterday; police have now come up with a suspect. The man believed to be responsible for the killing of Leonard Boston is Doctor Shawn Bomoski. We will have more on this crucial tragedy coming up tonight on channel seven action news. I'm Bill Bonds, bringing you the update news beat."

The cashier in the donut shop had no idea why Shawn placed five dollars on the counter so quick. "Are you leaving so soon? The dating game just came on," she said grabbing the money.

"Yeahhh, I just remembered I had some important business to take care of. You have a nice day Tammy, I'll be seeing ya," he said smiling.

"You to Shawn don't stay away so long next time."

"I want," he said rushing out.

"That's strange; he didn't even drink his coffee."

Shawn ran home as quickly as he could and when he got inside the house he gasped air trying to catch his breath. "I got to contact Mack: I got to get out this country. The police and news media goin be swarming all over the house in a minute." The answering machine came on, "damn, he got that damn answering machine on. Mack, this is Bomoski, contact me immediately, my life depends on you man."

Gena and Paula were just getting to Sharen's house and soon as they got inside, Sharen said, "there go grandma boy, granny missed that baby. How you been doing Gena?"

"I been doing okay mama."

"How bout you Paula, you enjoy being with your son? Sharen asked.

"Yeah mama, we had fun!"

"Well I'm glad you enjoyed yourself."

"Yeah I had a ball. Look mama the only reason I brought him back so soon is because my friend was killed yesterday."

"You're kidding, what was his name?"

"His name is Leonard Boston, he was a detective."

"Girl no, I just saw something about that on the news eat a few minutes ago, and they say they have a suspect."

"Did they give the suspect name?"

"Yeah they said his name was Doctor Shawn Bomoosk. I can't pronounce his last name, but it's something like that."

"Is it Bomoski?" Gena asked.

"Yeahhh that's it girl, Bomoski. They goin fry his ass, he killed a detective too, his ass is out!"

Paula and Gena looked at each other in shock. "That's my husband, I got to get back to the house!"

"Mama we gotta go," Paula said kissing her goodbye.

"I understand, y'all drive careful now, call me when you get'ah chance."

When they got in the car Gena said, "Shawn is in deep trouble, and he don't even know it. I can't believe he had something to do with Leonard getting killed. He was with us all day at the picnic, why would he wanna kill Leonard, it don't make no sense. Shawn is into something real deep; it don't take no genius to figure this out. Leonard must'ah had something on him, that's why Shawn had him killed. If they catch'em he goin spend the rest of his life in prison. What can we do about it Paula?"

"First we got to catch up with him before the police do. Then I guess he'll know what to do from there, just drive Gena, damn the speed-limit, and the police!"

When Gena and Paula got home they found Shawn sitting on the telephone. Gena looked at him, her voice trembling as she said, "what is going on Shawn? Your name is all over the news; is it true what their saying Shawn? Tell me it's not true!"

"I'm afraid it is Gena!"

Paula just shook her head, saying," why Shawn, what did he ever do to you?"

"Look, I don't have time to explain, I got to get out of here, Leonard should've stayed out'uv my business!"

"What business?" Paula cried out. "I wish you luck man because if the police ever catch up with you, they goin roast your ass. You in a lot'uv trouble Shawn!"

"Don't you think I know that? That's why I got to get out of the country for awhile. Gena, I'll let you know where I'm at as soon as I can, but right now it's best that you don't know."

Shawn kissed Gena goodbye and as soon as he opened the living room door, the police and news media were everywhere.

Gena couldn't believe what she was seeing as she watched the police throw her husband to the floor, guns pointed straight at his head.

Detective Sam was the first to speak saying, "you are under arrest you son-of-ah-bitch. You got the right to remain silent; any words you say could cost you your head. Get this dirt bag in'ah squad car."

Shawn didn't say a word, Gena and Paula stood by watching and crying. They didn't say a word until one of the officers asked Gena her name.

"I'm Gena Bomoski, I'm his wife."

"I would advise you to find yourself another husband ma'am because Shawn Bomoski may never see the light again!"

"My husband is innocent!"

"Save it for the judge miss, your husband is a killer!"

"Get those fucking cameras out my house, nowww!"

"Ma'am we're just getting started."

The police confiscated all the guns and pictures they found in Shawn's bedroom.

When they got Shawn down to the police station, Detective Sam did all the talking.

"Man, I know you wanna cooperate with me. I'm the only friend you have right now. Do you know what you're charged with man? You're charged with conspiracy to murder, buying guns illegal from an army base, and working as a doctor under an alias name, man we got your ass!"

Shawn yelled saying, "is that all you got on me! I wanna call my lawyer or is that against the law too?!"

"Oh you goin get'ah phone call. Here would you like a cigarette?"

"I don't smoke."

"How bout a cup of coffee?"

"All I want is my phone call!"

"Are those cuffs to tight? Here, let me take them off for you. I'm quite sure you want try anything and besides where would you run too!"

"I have no reason to run, I'm as innocent as you detective!"

"I'm sure you are Bomoski, now, let's get down to the real deal. I'm goin ask you some questions, and you goin answer them, you got that Mr. Bomoski?!"

"Please, call me Shawn."

"Okay Shawn, why did you have Leonard Boston killed?!"

"I didn't have Leonard Boston killed. Look detective, to save you some time, you ain't getting jack shit out'uv me. You're wasting your time and mines. I wanna see my lawyer before I say another word. Look man, I'm an innocent man, and that's all I know. Now if you don't mind I'll like to go back to my cell now!"

"I'll take you back to your cell, but I can promise you one thing!"

"And what's that detective?"

"I promise you, you goin pay for the death of my friend."

Shawn stared into the detective's eyes with an evil expression and said, "Detective, is that a promise, or is that a threat?!"

"You can take it anyway you want!"

"Well, right now it sound like'ah threat to me, and don't nobody threaten Shawn Bomoski's life and get away with it. Now that's a promise from me to you detective!"

Detective Sam's voice turned to rage as he yelled out, "do you realize how much trouble you're in man, and do you know that I'm the only one who can help your ass!"

"I'm not in trouble detective, and if I am, you best believe I can get out of it!"

"I don't think so not this time. Your ass is going down and I'm going to see to it that you do!"

"What you better do Sam, is watch the way you talk to me!"

Detective Sam reached across his desk and collared Shawn, saying, "are you threatening me boy? You are going to pay!"

They stared into each other's eyes with hate as Shawn said, "so are you Sam? Now, if you don't mind, let me go!"

As the detective let him go, Shawn thought to himself, "you one dead mothafucka, dead, dead, deadddd!"

"Take this piece of shit back his cell before I kill'em!"

As the officer handcuffed Shawn, Shawn said, "say detective, how bad you miss Leonard because I just ordered you a first class ticket to visit him!"

"Get his ass out of here before I do something I regret!"

The officer let Shawn make one phone call before taking him back to the ninth floor, and he called home. "Gena honey, this me, I only have a few minutes."

"Are you okay?"She asked.

"I'm fine baby, now listen to me, I want you to go in the bedroom and look in the dresser draw. You'll see a little black phone book; look on the first very page, you call that number. It's a lawyer number, his name is Tom Loeb, you tell'em that I need him right away. He'll know what to do from there. My time is up, I got to go now, don't worry about me baby. Everything's goin be all right, I promise!"

"I love you Shawn!"

"Got to go, I love you too!"

After Shawn hung the phone up the officer escorted him back to his cell on the ninth floor. Shawn just laid on his bunk thinking about all the mess he had gotten himself into. He was interrupted by a voice coming from the cell next to his cell.

"Yoe, my man next door, you got'a cigarette?"

"I don't smoke," Shawn answered.

"What they got you on man?"

"Some bullshit, what about you, what they got you on?"

"I killed four police officers in a shootout. I didn't even know they were cops. Bitches ran up in my joint, ain't said this the police or shit. Soon as my door flew open I started spraying everything in sight. Hell, I even shot at my damn self!"

Shawn laughed saying, "man you must'uv been high on some powerful shit!"

"N'all man I was in my right mind; just ain't goin run up in my house and I don't know who the hell they is!"

"I really can't blame you for doing that. I probably would'uv did the same thing if I was in your shoes. How many you say it was?"

"It wasn't but four of them."

"How did they catch you?"

"Hell, they didn't. I put all my dope up and called the police on myself. I told them four men just kicked my door in and tried to rob me. They came bringing me down here talking about I'm charged with first degree murder. I'm looking to walk on this sit. Number one they didn't have no reason to kick in my front door, and number two they didn't identify themselves, and number three I know a lil-something about the law."

"So how long you been down here?"

"I been here three days now. I'm still waiting to talk to homicide. After I talk to them I guess I go to court in the morning."

"Good luck man, I hope you beat that bullshit!"

"Yeah, me too. What did you say your name was?"

"I didn't say, and I rather not talk about my case to you. All I can tell you is they wanted me bad, but if you read the newspaper and watched the news, you'll know who I am, my name is Bomoski."

"You must be Italian with a name like that."

"I am Italian."

"Well if you're Italian I think I can just about guess what kind of trouble you're in my man."

"Don't bother trying, look, I'll holla at you in a few. Right now I'm about to catch a few zeez."

"Go ahead, I'm about to do the same damn thang."

Shawn dozed off to sleep. He slept for an hour before waking up, calling out to the cell next to his cell.

"Yoe, my man you up?"

"Yeah man, I ain't never went to sleep."

"Man you wouldn't believe the dream I just had. I had to wake up before I creamed in my pants."

An officer came to Shawn's cell saying, "come on Mr. Bomoski, you have an attorney visit."

"It's about damn time!"

When Shawn got inside the visiting booth with his attorney he said, "what took you so long?"

"It ain't been long ago I got your wife message. I didn't know you were married son. Now, I been busy talking to the judge, we are talking big bucks Bomoski!"

"You know money is no option, I don't care what it cost, get me the hell out of here!"

"No problem, I'll see you in court tomorrow, and I guarantee you'll walk out that court room a free man tomorrow, now you have a nice day."

"Yeah you too."

When Shawn got back to his cell he said, "you still over there my man?"

"Yeah man I'm still in this roach infested motha-fucka."

"Yeah man that was my lawyer who came to see me. He told me not to worry about nothing, he'll have me out of this dump tomorrow."

"Damn man, you must have a bad ass lawyer?"

"Yeah I do, you ever heard of Tom Loeb?"

"Hell yeah, that's one of the baddest attorneys' in the state of Michigan. I can remember when he got Appolonio Luse off all them murders, and he was guilty as hell. Tom Loeb is a bad boy, you got the best on your side, that's for sure. I wish I could afford his ass!"

"By the way, what's your name man?"

"My name Stone, Alvin Stone."

"I tell you what Stone, and I don't even know you, but I think you got'ah lot'uv heart. If you got enough heart to smoke another cop I'll get you out of here!"

"Man are you serious? I'll smoke three of them motha-fuckaz if you get me out of this hell hole. You just point him to me, he's a dead man, now who you want me to kill?!"

"His name is Detective Sam."

"Detective Sam, I can't stand that bastard no-way. He killed one of my boys not too long ago. Hell yeahhh, you got me out'uv here. I'll do that lil-job for you. I know some hell-able people out there!"

"I know you do, I treated a lot of patients that knew you. I heard your name many times before now!"

"So you're a doctor?"

"I'm known to be; let's just say I got just as much pull as the president."

"You're a powerful man then."

"Now here's the deal Stone: I get you out, you take care of that fake ass detective!"
"Can I ask you one question Bomoski?"

"What's that?"

"Why do you want this Detective Sam dead so bad?"

"Number one I don't like his slimy ass, number two nobody threatens Shawn Bomoski's life and gets away it. Number three I already told him I had a one way ticket for him to visit his dead friend in hell, and number four when I make a promise I always see it through so do we have a deal or not?!"

"Yeah man we definitely have a deal. When do you get me out of here?!"

"You go to court tomorrow don't you?" He answered, "so do I, and as soon as I get out, you get out. They got to give you a bond; it'll be a high one. They want be expecting you to make it and that's where I come in; there's no limit that I can't pay!"

Alvin thought to himself, "man, this man must be from Columbia. They're the only one with that kind'uv power or money."

"One more thing Stone."

"What's that Bomoski?"

"I hope you don't try and cross me when I get you out of here. I would hate to have to put a contract out on you, and this country ain't big enough to hide you, you feel me?!"

"Look Bomoski, right now I only can give you my word, and my word is my bond. You can trust me or you can say fuck me. It's all up to you; I know you are a powerful man in whatever you're doing. Now once you get me out of here, I'm only goin need one thing from you, and that's a forty-five glott with the silence that's all I want."

"That's no problem. When they release you, my office ain't far from here. I want you to go the Millender Center and tell the desk clerk you wanna see me. I'll leave word with her to give you a key to my office. You stay there till I get there. I'll have everything you need to get the job done when I get there. I have a feeling you and I goin become good friends if everything goes well with this job. Now if you don't mind I would like to get me some shut eye and think things over."

Meanwhile, back at the house Paula and Gena sat quietly watching television until Paula said, "Gena the baby crying."

"Sure is, I'll be right back, let me go get bad butt."

"While you're up there look in my purse and bring me a stick of gum."

"I hope its double-mint."

"It is you can have a stick too if you like."

"No kidding, listen to him. Mommy's coming, hold onnn."

After Gena changed the baby's diaper and picked him up. She said, "boy you almost made mommy forget Aunt Paula's gum."

Gena put the baby down and opened the purse up to get the gum, and spotted a piece of paper that looked like one of Shawn's checks, and said to herself, "this is one of

Shawn's checks filled out and signed. Ten-thousand dollars, why would Shawn make ah check out to Paula for ten-thousand dollars? They must be screwing or something. Paula wouldn't do that to me, it's got to be something else to this, I'll find out. I can't ask her anything about it, then she'll know I been rambling through her purse. I got enough on my mind already than to be worried about a check!"

Gena went on back downstairs, holding the baby in one arm and the gum in her free hand saying, "here's your gum."

"Thanks, it took you long enough."

"Girl I had to change his diaper."

"I need to change your diaper."

"I'm not wet honey."

"You will be when I'm finished with you," she said smiling.

"You think so?"

"I know so, put him down. I can show you better than I can tell you."

"I like the sound of that."

"All you got to do is get undressed."

"That's no problem, why don't you undress me."

"Oh I will," Paula said pulling Gena's pants off and placing her left leg over the sofa, and the other one on the floor, placing her tongue in the center of Gena's cherry.

"Damnnnn, Paula that feels good, make me cummm, that's it, suck that pussy."

"You like that?"

"Yes, yeahhhh, yeahhh Paula."

After they were done getting each off, Paula laid her head on Gena's breast and fell asleep. While Paula slept, Gena rubbed her hair and said, "Paula, I love you so much, I swear I do!"

April 10, 1973 9:00 A.M.

Shawn walked in the courtroom and stood before the honorable Judge Depurae. The deputy seated Shawn next to his attorney.

After the court clerk was done reading all the charges against Shawn, the prosecutor was the first to make his argument to the judge. "Your honor, you heard the charges being read against the defendant Mr. Bomoski. I think Mr. Bomoski is a threat to society, and with the charges in mind I believe the people will be satisfied if this vicious man received no bond!"

The judge cleared his throat and said," will the defense attorney be rebutting Mr. Power's argument?"

Mr. Loeb said, "yes your honor. In this country a man is not guilty until proven guilty, and my client pleads not guilty to all the charges brought up against him. He is an innocent man. This man I represent has spent all his life helping people in society; he's a doctor, and not a threat."

Paula and Gena walked in and took a seat in the front row behind Shawn.

"This man is no more threat to society than Mr. Powers himself is. I think a bond should be set for Mr. Bomoski today. Thank you your honor for hearing me out patiently, and for the said reasons I believe a bond would be appropriate for the defense!"

The judge took a sip of water from his cup. "Motion for bond granted!"

The prosecutor jumped out his seat and shouted. "Your honor I object, if this man is granted bond I think it should be no less than ten-million dollars!"

"I agree with you counselor, bond is met at one in a half million dollars."

"Thank you your honor," the prosecutor said smiling at Mr. Loeb.

"Next case please," the judge said.

Shawn smiled and whispered in his lawyer ear, "that ain't shit Tom."

"I know, do you want me to pay it, and you reimburse me later!"

"I'll be much obliged if you do that for me. I'll just give you two in a half million when I get out, and we'll call it even for now."

"Sounds good to me son, but don't forget, we got'ah lot of work ahead of us. Now, you just relax and I'll have you out'uv here in no time. Take care of yourself, and call me if you need me!

"I'll be sure to do that, take care Tom," Shawn said smiling.

"I'll tell your wife she can go on home. It's goin take awhile before they release you."

After Tom told Gena she could leave, her and Paula went straight home, and an hour later the phone ringed, and Gena answered. "Hello."

"Hi honey, it's me. I should be out in a couple'uv hours. Listen, this is what I want you to do for me, listen good now. Before you come down here and pick me up, I want you to stop by the bank and take out three million dollars."

"Three million dollars!"

"Yes, three million; just do what I ask you to do sweetheart. As soon as you hang up from talking to me, I want you call down here and find out how much is Alvin Stone's bond is, and whatever it is pay it. I got to go now; the police is telling me my time is up."

"Okay Shawn, I'll do that right now, I love you!"

"I love you too, see you after while."

As soon as Gena hung up, Paula asked, "who was that, Shawn?"

"Yeah that was him, he'll be out in a couple'uv hours he say. He wants me to pick him up, and bond some guy name Alvin Stone out. Let me call down there and see what his bond is."

Gena called the precinct. "First precinct, Sergent Dazz speaking."

"Yes, I would like to know are you holding an Alvin Stone?"

"Yes, we have an Alvin Stone here."

"Can you tell me if he has a bond or not?"

"Yeah sure, I'll have to check the computer first. Could you hold on for a second please?" Sergeant Dazz typed Alvin's name on the computer. "Thanks for holding on, Mr. Stone's bond is five-hundred thousand cash only."

"Thank you," Gena said hanging up. "Come on Paula, we got to get to the bank."

Ten minutes later Gena was pulling into the bank's parking lot. Paula said, "ooh Gena, I forgot to tell you Shawn gave me a loan. He said it should get me on my feet, and handed me a check for ten thousand big ones."

"That was nice of him; you might as well cash it while we're here."

"Might as well, that way I can give my mother half. I'm glad we're best friends; Shawn only gave me this money because of you. I hope you didn't mind."

"Of course I don't mind, I was planning on giving you some money myself he just beat me to the punch. Now let's get in there, we got business to take care of."

Shawn was released much earlier than he had anticipated, but he knew Gena would be coming down to thirty-six district court to bond Alvin out, so he waited for her there in the lobby.

Finally they arrived, Paula held the baby, and Gena held the money bag. As soon as Shawn spotted them he called out, "well it's about time."

"Shawn," Gena cried out then ran up and kissed him.

Paula smiled saying, "hi Shawn we missed you around the house doing nothing," they all laughed.

"I miss y'all too. Gena take care of that honey."

While Gena went to pay Alvin's bond, Detective Sam stepped off the elevator. He spotted Shawn and walked up to him saying, "I see you are a very important man around here Mr. Bomoski. I just want you to know one thing, I'm goin be on your ass like flies on shit, you got that, cop killer!"

"Detective Sam, you hear me, and hear me good; you're out your league when it come to fucking with me. I just hope your insurance is paid up cause somebody goin need some money to bury your soft ass. Now if you would excuse me, I got business to take care of!"

As Shawn walked away, Sam said," yeah I bet you do, I hope it's legal!"

Shawn turned around saying, "as a matter of fact it's not legal. Why can't you fuck with somebody in the minor league cause the big league goin cost you your life!"

"Cause I don't like assholes like you going around killing cops, especially when the cop is my best friend!"

"You want have to worry about that much longer. I arranged for you to take the same trip your friend went on, and detective that's not a threat, that's a promise!"

"Be seeing you Bomoski!"

"Come on y'all let's get the hell out of here. Did you take care of that?"

"Yes," Gena answered. "Who was that man you were talking too?"

"He's nobody, let's just go home now. I can use a good shower and a good meal."

Forty minutes later they were home and after Shawn got out the shower he ate a few burgers Gena had made for him while he was in the shower.

"Those hamburgers were delicious Gena. I got to make a quick run, I'll be back in a few," Shawn said smiling.

"Okay honey, be careful!"

"I will baby, now give me some sugar so I can be on my way," they kissed.

Shawn drove straight to his warehouse downtown where he kept his artillery and grabbed everything Alvin said he needed, then he drove straight to the Millender Center where he was to meet Alvin.

When Shawn got inside the Millender Center, he went straight to the desk clerk saying, "hi, any messages today?"

"No, but there is a Mr. Stone waiting for you in your office. I wouldn't have given him your key, but he said…" Shawn cut her off, "never mind the rest, you did good, thank you!"

When Shawn opened the door to his office he found Alvin's back turned staring out the window. Alvin said, "beautiful sight from up here Bomoski, I can see in Canada from here."

"Yes, it's quite a sight, and I see you are a man of your word!"

"Like I told you before Bomoski, my word is my bond. Did you get what I ordered?"

"If you get out of that window you'll see that everything is here."

Alvin turned around, and the five-foot-eleven, brown eyes, thirty-two year old, brown skinned man just stared at Shawn for a second.

Shawn said, "take a look in that bag Mr. Stone."

Alvin opened the bag real slow, and smiled saying, "well I'll be damned, you even got the silencer."

"I told you I'll supply everything you need, and like you Alvin, I'm also a man of my word. Just don't cross me!"

"Don't worry man, just give me a few days and you'll read about this in the newspaper!"

"I like yoe attitude Stone, I see we goin get along just fine."

"Look Bomoski, I'm a little shy on cash, and I..." Shawn cut him off.

"You must have bad eyes Stone? Take another look in that bag. Now there's twenty-five thousand dollars in there."

"For me man?!"

"Only if you want it."

"Damn Bomoski man, you too much. I couldn't cross you if I wanted too!"

Shawn just smiled, "here's my number where you can reach me and if you need for anything. I got to get going now; my wife is craving for me, if you know what I mean. You take care, be seeing you!"

Alvin watched Shawn walk out the door and said to himself, "you're a powerful man Bomoski, I got to stay on your good side, you can help me in many ways. I'll take care of that punk ass detective for you!"

April 11, 1973 9:15 A.M.

The next day Alvin got up and caught a Rocket cab to rent him a car. The 1972 red Mustang went good with the red leather two piece he had on.

As Alvin drove off the car lot he said to himself, "yeahhh this me, now all I got to do is get my own wheels. I think right now would be a good time to take that detective out, the earlier the better. Since I got a silencer I could waste his ass anywhere, but Bomoski want me to make sure he know he's the one behind all this."

Alvin drove straight to the police station and parked the car across the street in the Coney Island parking lot. He fixed his red leather hat on his head, and put on his dark sunglasses to hide his face. He checked the forty five glott to make sure the chamber was full, and said to himself, "come on Alvin Stone let's do this shit."

Alvin walked straight to the front desk where three police stood laughing and talking. Alvin interrupted saying, "yes, excuse me officers, I'm looking for Detective Sam's office."

One of the officers said," he's on the fifth floor, you can take the elevator or the stairs, it's your choice."

"Thank you man."

Alvin made his way to the fifth floor, and as he slowly walked the hallway he checked each name on the door.

"Bingo," he said as he stared at the name on Detective Sam's door, knocking four times.

"Come in," the voice said behind the door.

Alvin opened the door and walked in and said to himself, "good, he's alone."

Detective Sam was sitting in a black leather chair behind his desk. "Yes, what can I do for you sir?"

"My name is Stone."

"Sit down Mr. Stone, how may I help you?" He said puffin his cigarette.

"Actually Detective Sam, I'm here to do business with you!"

"What kind of business?"

"I have some information I think you'll be interested in, and this is not any old information."

"So Mr. Stone what do you want for this information?"

"Nothing involving money, see this man I met asked me to deliver a message to you. I believe he said is name was Shawn Bomoski!"

"Shawn Bomoski huh, what do you know about that bastard?!"

"Nothing really, only that he has a unique way of putting his words."

"What you mean? What did he tell you?" He said taking another puff.

"He told me to tell you that when Shawn Bomoski makes a promise, he never breaks it!"

"Well you can take this message here to him; you tell that son-of-a-bitch that I'm goin nail his ass to a tree if it's the last thing I do!"

"I don't think so detective, you see, I would love for you to tell'em yourself, but Mr. Bomoski has already ordered you a one-way ticket to hell, and I'm here to that you get there!"

Detective Sam reached for his gun, but before he could place his hand on it, Alvin's forty-five glott was staring him in the face. Alvin said, "I wouldn't do that if I was you detective. Now is there anything else you would like me to tell Mr. Bomoski before you die?!"

"You tell that slimy black bastard that I said to go!" Before Sam could finish his words, Alvin pulled the trigger shooting him right between the eyes. The impact from the glott threw the detective backwards. He landed face down on the floor.

Alvin turned him over, making sure he was dead, but he wasn't. "Damn, I see you're a die hard, lucky for me you are, this is for killing my boy!" Alvin fired two more bullets in the detective's head. "Don't forget to say hello for me."

Before Alvin could get six feet away from the detective office, an officer was headed his way. "Damn," he said to himself as the officer got closer to him. "Excuse me officer, could you show me where the bathroom is?"

"Sure, follow me, that's where I was on my way too anyway."

When they got to the bathroom, the officer turned around saying, "here we go son." Alvin's glott stared him in the face. "What are you doing?" He cried out.

"Just get yoe uniform wearing ass in there," Alvin shot the officer twice in the head and put his gun away. "Now you still full of shit!"

Alvin used the stairway to escape without being noticed. He drove to a nearby bar where he was known there for shooting pool and drinking beer. "I'll just chill out here for awhile, if anything goes wrong, I can always say I was at the Bronco Lounge all day drinking beer and shooting pool. Everybody know me here, the alibi is perfect."

(11:00 P.M.) Gena and Shawn were in bed watching television. Shawn had closed his eyes for a moment, but opened them when he heard the voice of Bill Bonds say, "our top story tonight, two officers were found shot to death at the downtown precinct. The bodies were discovered around eleven a.m. this morning. Both were shot multiple times in the head. There has been no suspect at this time, although police do believe that the same person who killed detective Leonard Boston is the same trigger man behind these two brutal killings. I'm Bill Bonds; I'll be coming to you live later on tonight at the first precinct, Carmen!"

"I'm Carmen Hollins for channel seven action news. Two boys were found floating in Lake Michigan today. Police and lifeguards are still searching the water for other bodies."

Shawn just smiled, thinking to himself, "Alvin Stone, you even had to kill another cop. I guess you earned that twenty five grand after all. You just earned yourself a job Mr. Stone. I believe I can make you a rich man with the kind of heart you got, I'll sleep good tonight. I wish I could have seen that bastard face when Alvin mentioned my name to his ass, what the hell, I got what I wanted."

"Gena are you sleep?"

After Gena didn't answer, Shawn turned the television off and joined her.

Friday, April 12, 1973 10:30 A.M.

The phone ringed waking everybody in the house up. Paula and Gena answered the phone at the same time. "Hello."

"Hello," they both said.

"Is Paula in?"

"I got it Gena. Hi, Mo what's up?"

"I was just calling to see if was still on for tonight."

"Yes, you can pick me up around nine."

"I'll see you around nine' then."

Back at the first precinct Lieutenant Hall walked into his superior officer's office saying, "look Captain, I want beat around the bush. You and I know that Shawn Bomoski is behind these killings. I say we go arrest that bastard before we lose another officer."

"I understand that you're saying lieutenant, but if you don't wanna be looking over your shoulder everywhere you go, you best leave Bomoski for the F.B.I., unless you wanna end up like Sam, Leonard, and that other officer. You better know who you're dealing with first!"

(Ten hours later) "Gena how do I look?"

"Girl you look lovely, don't she Shawn?" Gena said smiling.

"You sure do Paula, all royal blue. I like that royal blue silk dress: I even like your royal blue snake skin shoes, and you even got the purse to match. Why don't you and Gena have just one drink with me?"

Paula smiled, saying, "why not, I haven't had a drink in years. Come on Gena, one drink ain't goin kill you."

"Okay, just one," Gena said.

The doorbell sounded off, Shawn called from the couch. "Come on in Mo, can't be nobody but you."

Mo walked in smiling and said, "I see I'm just in time for a drink. Whyyy, Paula you look lovely!"

"Thank you, you look quite handsome tonight yourself."

"Now I'll drink to that, "Mo said smiling.

"We better get going Mo, the movie starts at nine-thirty," Paula said.

After the movie was over Mo drove Paula to the waterfront. He parked his Cougar on Jefferson Rd, and that's where they sat talking inside the car.

Mo gazed into Paula's eyes and said, "you know Paula, I didn't realize how beautiful you are until I saw you in this lovely dress tonight. Would you like something to drink? I have a little Scotch in the glove compartment."

"I would love one right about now."

"I'll make you one of my specials, you'll like this drink, I promise." Mo made the drink."Here, try this, it's a little sweet, but it's good."

"You know what Mo, you're much nicer than I thought. I guess you can't judge a book by its cover."

"I guess you can't. You know, I remember when my dad use to bring me down here to fish. I wasn't big enough to cast my rod out in the water so he would just let me play with my fishing rod. I miss those days!"

"Mo what did you put in my drink? Why I'm feeling so hot all'ah sudden. I think you put something in my drink!"

"Paula please, I wouldn't do nothing to hurt you."

"You did something to this drink!"

"Mo grabbed her by the arm saying, "why don't you bring yoe pretty self a little closer to me, I'll make you feel better!"

"Stop it Mo, don't do this to me!"

"Just come closer to me!"

"No, I feel so drowsy. I told you not to give me no drugs. I'm getting dizzier and dizzier. Stop it Mo, pleaseeeee… Stop it Mo, stop!" She cried out.

"Look bitch," he said pulling her by the hair. "I want you to get naked!"

"Mo please don't do this to me!"

Mo put his hand under Paula's dress and ripped her panty hose. Paula still crying as her mind flashed back to the time she was raped.

Mo took Paula's left leg and put it across the seat. "Please Mo!" She cried.

"Shut up bitch, I wish you wouldn't fight this, you want me hoe!"

"I'm begging you Mo, please don't do this to me!"

"Just don't fight it bitch. I'm fix'n to give you something you'll never forget!" He said unzipping his pants.

"Okay," she said with tears running down her face. "Here it is Mo, you know where to put it!"

"I knew you wanted it."

As Mo started stroking, Paula slid her hand into her purse filling around in it until she got a grip of the switchblade.

"You like this, don't you?" He said stroking.

"You like this?" She said slicing his throat with the switchblade.

Blood shot out his neck profusely as Paula pushed him off of her. Paula got out the car and ran across the street to the Coney Island restaurant screaming and crying out. "Somebody help me please!"

One of the waiters said, "oh my God somebody call the police. What happened miss? Here sit right here, the police are on the way. Did somebody attack you?!"

"I, I, killed a man," she cried out. "He raped me!"

"Just relax the police will be here in a minute."

"I need to call home."

"There's a phone over there."

"I don't have any money my purse is still in his car."

"Here, here's a dime," the waiter said. "Thank you."

Paula called the house and Gena could tell by her voice that something was wrong and asked, "Paula what's wrong?" Paula started crying even more. "Just calm down Paula and tell me what happened?"

"I, I, I think I killed Mo!"

"You what? God no Paula!"

The police officer walked up to Paula asking, "ma'am what on God's Earth have you done?" Another police officer walked in saying, "sergeant, we have a dead man across the street sir, it don't look good!"

"Ma'am you wanna come with me, I'll take that phone call for you; somebody cuff her." The sergeant got on the phone asking, "whom I'm speaking with?"

"My name is Gena."

"Well Gena, I'm with the Grosse Pointe Police Department, my name is Sergeant Allen, I'm afraid there's been a murder!"

"Oh my God!" Gena cried out.

"We're taking her to jail. You can come down if you like, but we have to charge her."

"I'm on my way," Gena slammed the phone down telling Shawn, "Paula's in jail!"

"What, in jail, for what?"

"She killed Mo, we got to go see'er. She's in jail and she sounded awful on the phone. I hope she's okay!"

"Yeah me too!"

Gena grabbed the baby; her and Shawn arrived at the jail rushing straight to the desk. "Hi my name is Gena Bomoski, I would like to know if you're holding Paula Jones?"

"Yes, we're holding a Mrs. Jones. I believe she's being photographed right now. You can see her when they're done."

"Can you tell me anything about what happened?"

"Yes, apparently she was raped by some pervert. I would'uv killed the bastard too. Here comes the sergeant now, he'll give you all the information you need to know about Mrs. Jones."

"Hi, I'm Sergeant Allen. You must be the lady I spoke with earlier on the phone?"

"Yes, I'm Gena, and this is my husband Shawn. Is she goin be all right?"

"Well, we have the name of the dead man; his name is Morris Smith."

"That's Mo all right," Shawn said.

"You guys know this man?"

"Yes, he was a friend of my husband."

"Well he's a dead friend now sorry, he was cut straight through the jugular vein. If I may ask, who is this lady to you two?"

"She's my best friend."

"You know that your best friend did the slicing!"

"She has a good reason, you can count on that. Mo probably gave'er some bad dope, knowing him!"

Shawn's eyes got big saying, "what, bad dope, what you mean bad dope?"

"I didn't want to tell you this about your friend; I had promised Paula I wouldn't, but Mo was the one bringing drugs in the center."

"Why didn't you tell me this before now? We may have saved that last girl!"

"I know, but I didn't want to break up y'all friendship. I'm sorry, I should'ah told you!"

Gena started crying and Shawn put his arms around her saying, "it's okay baby, I understand. I'll go see can we see Paula now. You just sit down and relax okay."

Shawn went to the desk, "excuse me, how much longer do we have to wait before we can see her?"

The fifty-two year old, dark eyes, five-foot-nine, corporal smiled saying," young man you have a long night in front of you. We have to transfer her to Wyandotte Hospital now, the lady has been raped. We have proper procedures we must follow. Also, the sergeant tells me they may have to pump her stomach; she's in bad shape right now. Why don't you take your wife and kid home, get some rest, and come back tomorrow. I'm sure y'all will be able to see her then."

"You have a good night corporal, we'll be back tomorrow." Shawn walked back to Gena. "Gena darling, there's no way we're gonna see'er tonight. They have to take her to the hospital first. We'll come back first thing tomorrow, don't worry!"

As Shawn and Gena walked away, the corporal called out, "drive careful."

"Good night corporal," Gena said.

After they had gotten in the car and started driving away, Shawn said, "you know Gena, all these years I've known Mo, I never could'uv guessed he was the one bringing dope into the center. Damn he played for a fool!"

"It's not your fault, you didn't know, I blame myself. I should've told you, maybe none of this would'ah never happened if I would'uv spoke up?"

"Now don't you go blaming yourself. Mo was my friend, but how can I feel sorry for a man who did what he did. That's why he was always calm when something happened at the center; he knew all the time what was going on. Now I know what really happened to my late wife; he was her supplier. My good friend Mo, you going to the right place. I'm quite sure hell has a bed waiting for his no good ass. If would'uv known before that he was the one giving my late wife that shit, he would'ah been a dead man. He deserved everything Paula did to his ass and more!"

"You shouldn't talk like that Shawn."

"I can't help it Gena. The more I think about those girls dying, the madder I get!"

"Please honey, try not to think about it. I just hope Paula pulls through this; this isn't the first time she's been raped!"

"You mean to tell me this is her second time being raped!"

"Yes, this has happened to her before. Her mind is probably a wreck. Damn, how could this happen to her, I thought they was out having a good time. I guess you can never tell what's going on in another person's mind."

"Yeah, I guess you're right about that. Well, home at last, we both better get some sleep. We have a long day ahead of us tomorrow."

"I'm not sleepy; I couldn't sleep right now if I wanted too."

Gena turned the television on, saying, "I guess I'll watch some T.V. eventually I'll fall asleep. You goin and get some sleep Shawn."

"Nope, I'm staying up with my wife."

Saturday, 9:00 A.M.

That next morning Gena called Grosse Pointe police station while Shawn lay sleeping soundlessly on the sofa. "Hello, you've reached Grosse Pointe police station, please hold, an officer will be with you in a moment."

"Damn answering machine," Gena said.

Seconds later, "Sergeant Turner speaking, how can I help you?"

"I'm calling about a Paula Jones you're holding in your jail. I would like to know if she can have visitors now."

"Yes ma'am anytime before eight o'clock tonight."

"Thank you sir!"

"You're welcome, have a good day."

Shawn woke up from the sound of the phone hanging up. Gena smiled, saying, "well good morning sleepy head."

"Good morning sweetheart, who was that on the phone?"

"I just called the police station to check on Paula. They said she can have visits anytime before eight tonight. I'm going upstairs to take a shower."

"Can I join you?"

"Sure you can, I'll make breakfast after we get out the shower and don't you forget to bring your rubber ducky."

After they were done romancing in the shower, Shawn said, "while you're making breakfast I guess I'll make a quick phone call."

"Don't be all day, not unless you like cold eggs."

"I won't, it'll only take a minute. You better check on the baby before you start breakfast."

Gena saw that the baby was sound asleep, and when she got downstairs her mind flashed back to the time her and Paula made love on the couch, and then it flashed back to the time they made love in the shower. Tears started falling from Gena's eyes as she said, "oh God, please don't let anything happen to Paula!"

"Meanwhile, Shawn was on the phone with Sorcerer. Sorcerer said, "I hope you have good news for me Shawn."

"Yeah, as a matter of fact I do. I have everything under control down here. I can't talk about it over the phone, I may be bugged. I'll be down your way next week. We can talk then!"

"Sound good, what day shall I be expecting you?"

"How about this Friday coming up?"

"Sounds good, I'll see you then, and by the way, my wife just gave birth to another child."

"Boy or girl?"

"Girl this time."

"Congratulations, I just might bring my son down and let him meet her."

"You do that, and bring the misses too," he said smiling.

"I'll do that, see you when I get there."

"Good day Shawn."

When Shawn got to Gena in the kitchen he said, "you been crying, what's wrong? It's Paula isn't it?"

"Yeah Shawn, I just can't get'er off my mind. I feel so sorry for her!"

Shawn put his arms around her. "Don't worry honey, Paula is a strong woman. She'll pull through this, now stop crying baby, she goin be just fine!"

While they stood embracing, the phone started ringing. "I got it, you just eat your breakfast before it get cold," she answered the phone. "Hello."

"Hi Gena."

"Paula, are you okay? I been worried sick about you. You don't know how happy I am to hear your voice. Are you all right, talk to me."

"Yeah I'm okay. He wouldn't listen; I kept telling him over and over don't do this to me, but he wouldn't listen. He started slapping me, calling me bitches, and all I can remember."

Gena cut her off, "don't talk about it, the important thing is you're okay!"

"I'm okay, just come and get me. They let me go this morning on a personal bond. I'll be waiting at the Grosse Pointe police station."

"Okay, we're on the way."

"Was that Paula?"

"Yeah that was her. They let'er out on a personal bond; we got to go pick her up."

""That's good, a personal bond. See I told you she would be okay. Let's go get'er. I'm taking you two on a trip with me this weekend. A friend of mine has invited me to his home this Friday coming up. I told him we would be there."

"A trip sounds wonderful, who's the friend?"

"His name is Sorcerer."

Gena thought to herself, "I knew I knew that voice on the phone from somewhere. He used to call Antonio all the time and I would listen on the other phone to them talk. I never saw him in person, now I'll finally get the chance to meet the man behind the voice."

"I'll like to meet this Sorcerer."

"Well you'll get your chance to meet him this Friday."

One hour later they were at the jail. Paula was just getting ready to get back on the phone until she heard a voice behind her saying, "we're here." Paula slammed the phone down and ran straight to Gena saying, "what took you guys so long? I was just about to call the house. I'm so happy to see you girl!"

Shawn smiled saying, "now you two just cut it out."

"Hi Shawn, it's good to see your face too."

Shawn held the baby up in his arms and said, "Antonio missed you too."

Paula smiled saying, "alllll come here you little pumpkin, auntie missed that baby, yes auntie did. I'm starving let's go get something to eat. I'm so hungry I could eat a cat; I haven't had a bite to eat. They had these tubes in my arms all night."

Gena just smiled saying, "come on girl, let's go get you something to eat. When do you go back to court?"

"I believe the judge said November 6th; that's seven months from now. Whew this boy getting heavy."

Shawn took them to Bonanza Restaurant and while they sat eating Shawn said, "Paula how would you like to go on a trip with Gena and I this weekend?"

"I would love too, where we going?"

"We're going to Columbia."

"You're kidding, I always wanted to go there just couldn't afford it."

"Well you can afford it now, this one is on me. You and Gena will enjoy y'all selves there."

"What about you honey, I know you goin enjoy yourself too," Gena said.

"No not really, I'm just going strictly for business only. For all I know the telephones at the house could be bugged; that's why I'm flying out to Columbia. After that thing went down with Leonard, the police will be doing all they can to get me!"

Gena said, "please y'all, can we find another subject to talk about?!"

Friday April 19, 1973 2:00 P.M.

Mack landed the jet in Columbia airport. Sorcerer's chauffeur was there to meet them and twenty-minutes later they were entering Sorcerer's mansion.

Sorcerer greeted them at the front door as he listened to Paula saying, "Gena, I can't believe my eyes. Would you look at the size of this place, girl this man has to be filthy rich."

Sorcerer just smiled, holding his hands in the air saying, "Shawn Bomoski, it's always been a pleasure to have you here. Do come in, how was the flight?!"

"Smooth as always, you know Mack."

"Well, well Bomoski you haven't aged a bit," he said smiling.

"And neither have you. I would like you to meet my lovely wife Gena, and this is her best friend Paula, and this little fellow is Antonio."

"You have a beautiful family Shawn."

"Speaking of family, where is Maria and the kids?"

"Oh they are around here somewhere. If you all will come this way I'm sure we'll run into them. How's the weather back in Detroit?"

"Not as good as the weather down here," Shawn said smiling.

"I see your son likes to sleep."

"Yeah he gets his share."

"Well one of these days he'll be as powerful as you."

"I hope so those are my plans; after all somebody will have to run our business one day might-as-well be our sons. You're looking at the next Shawn Bomoski; little Antonio here is going to be as successful as me one day!"

"You know I use to have a Antonio who worked for me."

Gena thought to herself, "yeah you're the man who had him killed. If you didn't give a damn about Antonio, I know you don't give'ah damn about Shawn. One day somebody goin fill you up with bullets and I hope I live to see that day!"

Sorcerer changed the subject. "So Paula, are you married?"

"Nope, I'm single as a shingle."
"A woman as beautiful as you should have a husband; someone to take care of you in this wonderful world."

"I guess you can say I'm one of the unfortunate ones," she said smiling.

"Don't talk like that; I'm sure the right man will come along. So Gena, how are you enjoying the married life?"

"I'm enjoying every moment of it; actually this is my second marriage. My first husband was murdered!"

"Murdered; I'm so sorry to hear that. Well, I hope your second marriage with this man last a lifetime."

"So do I," Gena said smiling.

Maria had her back turned playing with her baby when Sorcerer opened the door saying," now in this room we will find my wife. Maria darling," he called.

Maria said, "what is it? Ohhh I see we have company."

"You remember this man here?"

Maria smiled saying, "hi Shawn, how long has it been? You haven't changed a bit."

Maria this is Shawn's wife Gena and their friend Paula!" Sorcerer said.

"Nice to meet you both," Maria said smiling. "And who is this lil-fella?"

"This lil-fella is my son Antonio," Gena said smiling.

"He's so cute, come over here with me, I'll show you my baby. This is my daughter her name is Tamara."

"Oh isn't she cute," Paula said smiling.

"Oh, she's a doll. She's so pretty, look at the pretty ribbons in her hair," Gena said smiling.

"Maybe one day, you Antonio, marry my Tamara," Maria said smiling.

Paula laughed saying, "who knows anything is possible. This could be your future son-in-law."

Gena smiled saying, "well one thing about it, we have a long time to wait before that day come."

Sorcerer said, "come on Shawn, let's leave these ladies alone for awhile. I have some good Scotch on us. Is that still your favorite?"

"You know it, and I could use a drink right about now."

"Maria we'll be at the bar. You two ladies just make yourself at home and relax your minds," Sorcerer said smiling.

When Sorcerer got to the bar he played the bartender and fixed him and Shawn a drink saying, "Shawn, as long as I have known you, you have always kept a level head. You always think before acting; I just wanna know one thing."

"And what's that?"

"I'll like to know how in the fuck do you bring somebody to my house without consulting with me first!"

"I'm sorry man, you're right. I should've told you I had somebody else coming with me. It won't happen again!"

"I hope not; I would hate to end our relationship!"

"Now wait'ah minute Sorcerer, what you trying to say?!"

"I'm not trying to say, I'm saying, you keep slipping up like you're doing I'm goin cut you off," Sorcerer's voice turned into rage. "First you order a hit, I send you two men, and look what you do. You give them a fuck'n tape to play that could cost both our futures; then you bring this bitch to my home without telling me shit. You slipping Bomoski!"

"I said I was sorry; I'm not goin jeopardize our business!"

"You better not, cause I'll have your head on a silver platter before you could blink an eye!"

"It won't happen again!"

"You're a good man Bomoski, but I want hesitate to kill you. Do I make myself clear!" He said sipping his drink.

"Are you threatening me?!"

"No Bomoski, I'm not into threatening people, but what I say stands. I made you Bomoski; I gave you your first start. Don't you forget where you came from!"

"How can I when you do all the thinking and talking?"

"Look Bomoski, I just don't want you to get careless, that's all. When we start getting careless we allow all sorts of unnecessary doors to open. We can't afford that, now do you understand me!"

"Yeahhhh I understand!"

"I like you Bomoski, but don't ever forget who made you!"

"I'll never forget where I came from. You've known me all my life; you know I'm loyal to you. Once again, I apologize for my stupidity!"

"Bomoski you are a man of many words, I accept your apology!" Sorcerer held his glass in the air. "A toast to you and your new family." They touched glasses downing their liquor. "So Bomoski, I have a big shipment coming your way. I want you to be on top of things!"

"No problem, how big is the shipment?"

"its street value is estimated to be six-billion and that's why I want you to handle everything. You and I can own this world one day at the rate we're going. We need a few more good men in your United States to help us out."

"I have just the man for us; he done some work for me back home. He's good at what he does; he works like a professional."

"Have I ever heard of this man you speak of?"

"You may have, his name is Alvin Stones. He's a man of his word and he don't waste time."

"I want you to contact this Stone person and give him a job."

"I'll do that as soon as I get back home. The real reason I flew here today; I had another detective killed. He had pictures of you and me; he wanted me bad. He would've caused a lot of problems for us!" He said sipping his drink.

"Am I hearing you right Bomoski? You say the police have pictures of me in their possession?!"

"Yeah, but they're not on to you."

"And how do you know that Bomoski? How can you guarantee me the F.B.I. want be kicking my doors in next? Those pictures could cost my life!"

"Don't worry; those pictures will never make it to court, trust me. I'll take care of everything as soon as I get back to Detroit, that I promise you. Now, when do this shipment come in?"
"Wednesday," he answered.

"Well Thursday, I want you to turn your satellite on. I'm about to make some noise in the big city; just make sure you pick up channel seven!"

"I'm counting on you Bomoski."

"I know and I want let you down!"

Monday April 22, 1973 2:00 A.M.

Maria hated to see Paula and Gena go home. The three of them had gotten to know each other very well.

Maria smiled saying, "Gena, Paula, you two come back soon, I enjoy company."

Paula smiled saying, "if she don't, I sure am."

Gena laughed saying, "we'll be back, but you goin have to come visit us too. You say you never been to America, you'll love it."

"Maybe one day my husband will bring me," Maria said smiling.

Sorcerer's chauffeur drove them to the airport where Mack awaited them.

Twelve hours later they were back home, and the first thing Shawn did walking through the front door was call the Millender Center hoping Alvin had left him a message. "Yes, Shawn Bomoski, any messages for me?"

"Yes Mr. Bomoski, you have one message. An Alvin Stone said you can reach him at 933-3393. He also said for me to tell you that you are a hard man to catch up with."

"He said that huh, thanks Sherry, talk to you later."

"Good day Mr. Bomoski."

Shawn dialed the number Sherry gave him. "Yeah Alvin speaking."

"A hard man to catch up with huh?"

"Bomoski my man; man share where the hell you been. You're a hard man to track down. A man like you should stay in touch with a man like me. I still have some of that money you gave me, but it's getting kind of low if you know what I mean!"

"Look Alvin, never mind that chump change. How would you like to make some real cash? Be in charge of your own lil organization!"

"Shawn my man you are talking my kind of talk. Ain't nothing in this world I love more than money my man!"

"I can make you a rich man Stone; meet me at my office tomorrow at twelve noon my friend."

"You couldn't have caught me at a better time, I'll be there. I can't wait to see what's on the menu this time. See you tomorrow, you have my word on that!"
"Good then I will see you tomorrow, don't be late goodnight Alvin."

"It is now Bomoski take care," Alvin hung the phone up and shouted. "Hot damn I'm fix'n to get rich. I knew I had the right man on my side. Bomoski has pull and I'm willing to bet a million dollars against one that him and Sorcerer is on the same line, and they have caught the right fish. Hell I can goin spend these lil seven thousands up. Lookout Detroit, Alvin Stone is back again. You can't keep a good man down for long even though these punk ass police are trying too!"

Tuesday April 23, 1973 12:00 Noon

Alvin sat on the desk while Shawn sat back in his black leather chair explaining his plan. "Look Alvin, I won't beat around the bush since I think I can trust you. I have billions of dollars worth of dope coming in tomorrow; six billion to be exact. I will give you five million dollars worth to do whatever you want with it!"

"What exactly do I have to do to earn this type of deal?"

"This deal is better than the first one you done for me. The only difference is you'll need a posse this time. I would say about eight good men who know what they are doing. Now here's the deal, you may not know this, but I'm into the biggest drug industry in America, and let's just say the law has some evidence that just might bury my ass!"

Alvin smiled, "and just how do you expect me to get this piece of evidence that could bury your ass?"

"I don't expect you to get anything; all I want you to do for me is to take the first precinct off the map. No precinct, no evidence!"

"And how do you expect me to do that, I don't…"

Shawn cut him off, "just be cool and listen. I'm goin make sure you have everything you need to get the job done. All you have to do is find some men to help you pull it off. A man of your abilities, I'm sure that's no problem for you!"

"Consider it done Bomoski!"

"That's what I wanted to hear. I need this done no later than Friday. I have a warehouse down here. It's only blocks away; it's the Hudson Warehouse. You can't miss it. It's right off Griswold Street."

"I know where it is."

"Good, when you get there you'll find everything you need," Shawn handed Alvin a bag with a hundred thousand dollars in it. "Here's a little something for showing up on time. I'm goin make you a rich man Alvin Stone, remember, no later than Friday. Once the job is done get back with me right here. I'll pay you what I owe you. You're my number one man Alvin; anything you need you see me, I mean anything. Here's the key to the warehouse. You have a good day Alvin and don't spend all that money in one place. Oh, here's my card, it has my pager number on it; contact me once you're done."

"You got it," Alvin said as he watched Shawn leave out the door. "This is going to be exciting. Let me get on my job. I know just the man to get to help me pull this shit off. It don't take no genius to figure out, I got to pay somebody to help me. What the fuck, I can afford it." Alvin flipped through the bills, smiling as he stared at the money. "Damn and I didn't even have to kill for this money. A man with your kind of money Bomoki can have anything done. Money is power as power is money. Let me get my ass out of here, I got work to do. I know just where to go my boy Dino; he's the leader of the Ecorse Gangsters. We're like brothers; they're known for blowing up shit."

"Alvin drove straight to Wayne Foss's car lot. "Yoe my man how much is this Lincoln here?"

The car dealer said, "that's a rich man's car son. Niggas can't afford this kind'uv beauty boy, but she'll go for twenty thousand now what you're looking for is right over here."

"N'all my man, what I'm looking for is right in front of my eyes. Now if you don't mind Uncle Tom, I'll take this car right here!"

The six-feet, black eyes, brown skinned car dealer just laughed saying, "well come on in this office. I'll have you in that new Lincoln in a heartbeat. I hope you got a good damn credit card and a few thousands in your pocket."

"I see all you niggas like to do everything but ya job. What would you say if I just gave you a nice even twenty-six thousands? Being that there is a such thing as the I.R.S. if you catch my drift."

"I would say you got yourself a brand new Lincoln Continental, and I'll make sure the I.R.S. stay home."

Alvin just smiled and paid the man and said," you mind if I leave this rent-a-car here for a few hours?"

"Oh no, go right ahead," he smiled.

Alvin got in the Lincoln as he drove off heading for Ecorse to find Dino, and as he drove he said to himself, "one of these days I'm goin own my own car lot. From here on out I'm living large. I want the best of everything; best food, best women, best cars, etc. Hell I wanna see when they kill the snakes and the alligators when I buy my shoes. I wanna be able to walk in my backyard and pull the lobsters and the catfish right out of my own lake. The whole world goin know who Alvin Stone is. Al Capone ain't goin have shit on me."

When Alvin got to Ecorse he drove down 13th Street and pulled in front of Dino's house. Dino and some of his friends were sitting on the front porch. They watched the brand new Lincoln come to a stop.

Dino took a sip from his sixteen ounce Budweiser beer and said, "I wonder who the hell this is in front of my crib. Y'all get ready I don't like the sight of this shit!"

Alvin let the tinted window on the passenger side down and yelled out, "I see you ain't changed boy!"
Dino recognized the voice. "Mannn that's my boy Alvin," he said to his boys. "I see you ain't holdin'em up," he said walking to the car.

"You know me Dino, ain't nothing changed, get in man, I got'ah talk to you," he said smiling.

Dino turned around and said to his boys," don't drink all the beer," and he got in the car. "So man when did you get the wheels?"

"Today lil-brother, I left my rent-a-car on the lot. I still got a month to go before I turn it in. I want you to go with me to pick it up. You can drive it and turn it in when the time expires."

"I ain't got no problem with that. Damn Alvin, it's good to see your ass. I thought you were doing time for wasting them polices."

"Oh you heard about that?"

"Yeah man, you know news travel fast around here."

"Don't worry about that; the important thing is I'm here, live in the flesh. Now this is what I want to talk to you about. What you doing this Friday?"

"I ain't doing nothing Friday, not unless you got something up."

Alvin threw ten-thousand dollars in Dino's lap saying, "I need your help man!"

"What's this for man?"

"It's yours; it's for being my lil-brother. You know I love you boy!"

Dino smiled saying, "what you need me to do?"

"Well actually I need you and your boys. It's twenty-five G's for each man you bring with you and a hundred thousand for you if you help me!"

"Man cut the bullshit you know I'm goin help your ass. Now what you want me to do?!"

"I need you to get eleven of your gangsters together, meet me tomorrow night at nine o'clock at the Hudson Warehouse Downtown. When you get there Dino, we have a building to take off the map. I got everything we need at the warehouse to blow this mothafucka off the face of this earth."

"Don't worry I'll be there!"

"My man, I knew I could count on you. Here's the key to the rent-a-car, it's the red Mustang parked over there."

"Damn, I see you love you some red; red Mustang, red Lincoln, I even remember that red Cougar you drove."

"Yeah, I love my red. You know you got enough money in your pocket to buy any car you want off this lot."

"Pockets do got the mumps," he said getting out the car. "I already got'a car," he said smiling.

"No you don't."

Dino held the key in the air smiling. "Yeah I do, and don't forget to call it in stolen."

"Still into that tagging shit I see."

"Yepp, ain't nothing changed; different strokes for different folks."

Alvin just laughed and drove off saying to himself, "that boy ain't got'ah bit of sense. I'm goin put you down with me when I get my share of the yae-o. We goin have Ecorse and River Rouge sowed up; ain't shit goin be able to touch us Dino. Everybody goin know your brow eyed ass. I'm thirty-two you thirty; by the time you get thirty-two you'll be untouchable. We got the right man backing us up; we'll never be broke again. I guess I'll have my house built in Romulus, this way I can have my lake built in my backyard. Hell who knows, I might even get married. N'all I don't need no bitches slowing a player like me down. I screw around too much to get married. My wife probably would come home and catch me in bed with two hoes and kill my black ass. I guess I'll stay single. I wonder what happens to that crazy ass broad that gave me the pussy then start crying rape like me and my boy took the panties. She was a fine ass chick though I have to admit it. The cherry was good as hell; hope I never run into that nut again she probably still strung out on that shit. Bitch actually gave up the sex and then hollered rape. I'm glad no police was around; my ass would still be doing time. Guess I'll stop here at J.R. Lounge for a minute since I'm out."

As soon as Alvin got inside the bar, Frank the bartender called out, "Alvin my man, long time no see. What will it be the usual?"

"Yeah Frank, you know me, got to have my Budweiser, and Frank, see what the lady on the other end is drinking. Whatever it is giv'er two."

Frank smiled saying, "I see you ain't changed son."

Frank was an older man than normal bartenders and a strong black man to be sixty years old. He thought of Alvin like a son and was always trying to give Alvin advice. Alvin respected Frank like he did all his elders.

"Alvin my son," Frank said smiling. "The lady asked me to invite you down."
"Well you know me old man, can't keep the lady waiting," he said smiling.

Alvin got his beer and walked down to the other end of the bar where the lady dressed in blue waited for him. Her smile caught Alvin's eye as he said smiling, "you have a beautiful smile. I'm sorry; I didn't mean to be rude. My name is Alvin, what's yours?"

"My name is Honey. Thank you for the drinks," she said smiling.

"You're more than welcome. Honey huh, now that's most definitely a sweet name. Are you as sweet as your name?"

"It depends on your taste bud."

"I like your style, look, why don't we go somewhere else where it's nice and quiet like sayyyy my house."

"That sounds good to my ears too. Is your last name Stone?"

"Yes it is. Does that change anything Ms. Honey?" He said smiling.

"Nope, but I heard so much about you Alvin."

"Why don't we leave now, that way I can tell you some more about me." Alvin helped Honey put her leather coat on, and threw twenty dollars on the bar.

Frank grabbed the money saying, "I ain't never seen'ah man so smooth. Bitches love that young nigga. Oh well some men have it, some men don't." He watched Alvin leave out the door and yelled out, "save some for pops."

Ten minutes later Alvin was pulling into his driveway, "Is this your house?" Honey asked smiling.

"Yeah, this is my house. I hope to own something much bigger than this one day soon."

"This house is nice looking on the outside."

"Oh if you like the outside, you goin love the inside. It's so warm and cozy on the inside," Alvin rubbed his hand across Honey's cheek. "Almost as warm as you."

"Is that right?"

"That's right baby, I can't wait to get inside your house. I know it's warm in there," he said smiling.

"Well the door will soon be opened as you got the key to my lock baby."

When they got inside the house Alvin turned the radio on asking," would you like something to drink? I have plenty beer and liquor."

"Do you have any gin?"

"Yepp as a matter of fact I do. Why don't you kick back, make yourself at home while I pour us a drink."

After a few shots of gin Alvin talked Honey into coming into his bathroom. Alvin put his robe on and said, "you goin leave me in this big oh waterbed by myself?"

"I don't think so," she said taking off her clothes.

Alvin looked at her well put together frame, and as she slipped out her dress Honey smiled saying, "you like what you see?"

"You know I do baby, now just bring your sexy self on over here so I can touch you in all the right spots," Alvin thought to himself as he watched her get in the bed. "I'm goin tare this pussy up."

Honey sat her cherry right on Alvin's cucumber. Alvin rolled her over on her back and slid his cock into her hairy nest. She moaned desperately for him to stroke harder, and the more she moaned, the faster he stroked.

Alvin unloaded inside of her, and slowly took his cucumber out. Honey protested, "please Alvin baby, you got to let me relax a minute. My stuff is sore as hell. I see you know how to work that dick."

Alvin just stared at the ceiling not saying a word. His mind was on the job he had to do for next day.

Honey went straight to sleep. Alvin looked over at her and smiled saying to his self, "yeah you just another bitch to me."

Alvin nodded off and he when he woke up he looked straight at the clock, and then turned to Honey shaking her a few times and saying at the same time, "get up baby, it's time to go."

"What time is it she asked?"

"Time for you to get dressed, party is over."

"Yeahhh all you men's are just alike. Get what y'all want, and treat a woman like shit!"

"No, no sweetheart, I'm not treating you like shit. If I was doing that I'll make your ass walk home at one in the morning. Now goin get dressed before I decide to do just that!"

226

Alvin and Honey got into the red Lincoln. Alvin said, "where you live anyway?"

"I stay on Holford Street, that ain't nowhere from here."

Alvin smiled, "well you wouldn't have had far to walk if I would'uv put you out."

"You would'nah made me walk home for real would you?"

"N'all baby I wouldn't do that to you. I got more respect than that for a woman. Well this is Holford, what house you stay in?"

"I stay in the second block."

Alvin got to the second block saying, "tell me when to stop."

"Right there, the second house off the corner."

Alvin stopped the car and said, "I had a great time Honey."

Honey opened the door asking, "when will I see you again?"

"Are you kidding, any female that give up her body on the first day she meet'ah man can't be about shit."

Honey tried to hold the car door open to say what she had to say, but Alvin pulled off. She screamed out as the car drove away. "You ain't shit nigga; I know twelve year old who fuck better then you, you bastard!"

Alvin could see Honey standing in the middle of the street cursing through his rearview mirror, and said to himself, "that chick is crazy as hell. Hope I don't run into her again no time soon. I got'ah stop treating women like this, all I do is lov'em and leave'em.

As Alvin drove down Schaefer Road he spotted a white lady being attacked by three black thugs, and said to himself, "all this pussy out here, these three niggas got'ah take some. I can't let it go down like that. Three against one ain't never been'ah fair fight."

Alvin stopped the car halfway up the block from the incident, and got out and popped the trunk putting the silencer on his thirty-eight revolver. Alvin slammed the trunk close and walked in a fast pace towards the sound of the screaming coming from the lady's mouth.

The thugs had forced her into the alley behind the hardware store on the corner of Ethel Street. When Alvin got to her they had already tore most of her clothing off. Alvin stared at them for a second before saying, "you boys having fun?" Alvin had his gun behind his back gripped tight. "Let the lady go!"

One of the thugs pulled out his switchblade saying, "nigga you better get you some business, I'll kill this white trash."

"I don't think so," Alvin said bringing the gun from behind his back. "Oh now I really got y'all attention. That's right nigga; get your punk ass off her. Three grown ass men against one lil helpless woman!" All three men stared into Alvin's eyes. "Miss you can get up, they not goin bother you no more. Now you boys consider today y'all lucky day.

I'm not goin send y'all to hell this time, but I'm goin send y'all to the hospital. Let me show y'all how it feels to be fucked by'ah steel dick!" Alvin shot all three men in the groin and smiled. "Didn't know you fellas could scream like bitches. When y'all had nuts y'all didn't know what to do with them. Come on miss, let me get you home!"

"How can I thank you, you saved my life!" She said trying to fix her shirt.

"You can thank me by staying off these streets so late at night. These men on this side of town are dangerous miss!"'

"My name is Lora, I been catching the bus for years at that bus stop and this has never happened."

"First time for everything Lora, I suggest you stop catching the bus and get you a car. Now where do you stay?"

"I stay on the other side of Jefferson on Maple Street."

"I know where that's at, I'll drop you off."

"What's your name?"

"My name is Alvin Stone."

"I'm glad you came along when you did Alvin!"

"Yeah me too, I can't stand men like that. Me and my thirty-eight showed them; you ain't gotta worry about them thugs no more."

"What makes you think that?"

Alvin started laughing saying, "because they ain't got no more dicks. They lost their virginity tonight back there. Well Lora, this is Maple Street, what block you stay in?"

"This one right here, slow down just'a little, right....here."

Alvin stopped the car, "good night Lora, and buy you a car."

"Thanks for everything Alvin. Would you like to come in, maybe have a drink or something? It's the least I can do for the man who saved my life!"

"N'all not tonight, it's been a long day for me, maybe some other time."

"Well you know where I stay now feel free to drop by anytime, I'm single."

"I'll keep that in mind, goodnight Lora." Alvin watched her open her front door, and then slowly pulled off, thinking to himself, "damn, what'a night. I got to take my ass home and get some sleep."

Wednesday April 24, 1973 6:00 P.M.

Shawn pulled into the parking lot of West Grand Blvd Park where he always parked waiting on the shipment to come in. Shawn scanned the scenery saying to himself, "I don't see no unfamiliar boats around and no unmarked police cars. Everything is going smooth as usual. It's time to load you up old Betsy," a name he'd given his station wagon the first day he bought the car.

Shawn went abroad the large ship and one of the workers said, "what's up Bomoski?"

"Hey Red, how's everything?"

"Just fine sir."

"That's good, say Red, when you start unloading, how bout putting ten of those bundles in my car for me."

"No problem, have you ready in no time."

Shawn sat at the railing of the ship and watched Red and his crew unload the yae-o. His mind was on Alvin as he focused his attention on the men below him. "Alvin you are a good man; I ain't never met a man like you with so much heart. I know you will be real successful in the drug business, just don't turn your back on me when you make it. You're too smart to piss on me; at least I hope you are. I'll have a long talk with him just to see where his mind is."

Red walked up to Bomoski saying, "hey boss, everything is set up to go. You want us to deliver it to the usual spot?"

"Yeah, if anything goes wrong you know what to do. I'm out'uv here."

Shawn drove the ten bundles of dope straight to his storage room that he bought from an oriental couple. Back in the late 50's Shawn tried to buy the couple out, but they wouldn't sell. Instead of selling they let him buy two storage rooms that he often uses.

When Shawn got to the storage he quickly unloaded the yae-o into the storage room and said to himself, "well Alvin this is where yoe five million worth'a dope goin be when you complete your mission. All you got to do is pick it up. I'm sure you ain't goin have no problem with that. I hope its a thousand police in the building when you blow it up. I can't stand cops, never could, and never will. I remember when those dirty mothafuckas killed my baby brother. Shoot'em in the head twice and told my mother he shot himself; he could'na did no shit like that if he wanted too. If he wasn't for them my brother would still be living today. I have no sympathy for'ah punk ass police. I better get going. I know Gena wondering where I'm at. I'll stop at a payphone and call'er."

Shawn spotted a payphone and pulled to call home. Paula answered the phone, "hello."

"Hi, Paula, put Gena on."

"It's your husband," Paula said.

Gena grabbed the phone, "Shawn, where are you?"

"I'm on my home now, baby what you cook for dinner?"

"I made pepper steak and rice. While you out there pick up some olives."

Shawn laughed, "you ain't pregnant are you?" He still laughed.

"That's not funny, no, but I feel like I am."

"I was just joking honey, I'll be home shortly."

"You better," she said hanging up.

When Shawn got home he found Gena and Paula lying on the floor playing with the baby. Gena looked up at him and said, "well it's about time, your dinner is on the stove."

Gena followed Shawn in the kitchen saying, "me and Paula was just talking about going shopping tomorrow. Would you like to come with us?"

"That sounds like a good idea, I would love too. What you thinking about buying yourself?"

"I saw this mink coat in the newspaper today, and I think it would look good on me," she said smiling.

"I know you would look good in that mink coat. I mean you already look good; that mink coat will look good on you. Yeahhh that's what I'm trying to say."

"Get it right," Gena said smiling.

Shawn put his arms around her saying, "I have it right sweetheart. There's no fur or jewelry that could compare with the beauty I see in you. I'm a very lucky man to have you. I love you more than anything in this world Gena!"

"Will you show me tonight?!"

"I sure will baby."

"I can't wait," she said walking away heading to the living room smiling, "I see you rocked oh bad butt to sleep."

"Yeahhhh he's out of it."

"Why don't you take'em upstairs. I'll be right behind you all the way."

Paula took the baby upstairs, Gena trailed right her, and when Paula bent over to put the baby in the crib, Gena rubbed her hands across Paula's ass. Paula smiled saying, "girl don't get nothing started you can't finish."

Gena put her arms around Paula's waist saying, "I love you Paula."

"I love you too Gena."

"Kiss me then."

"Girl what about your husband?"

"Don't worry about him, he's eating right now."

The two of them laid on the floor, and as soon as Gena got ready to undo Paula's blouse, Paula said, "I hear something."

"That's Shawn," Gena said. "Quick get dressed."

"Damn Gena, I told you not to start nothing you couldn't finish; got me all wet for nothing."

"Sorry, let's go downstairs and watch some television."

"Gena!" Shawn called out.

"Be right there," she shouted and ran downstairs. "Did you enjoy your dinner honey?"

"Yeah baby, I'm full as hell. I'm fix'n to go upstairs and take a quick nap."

"Go right ahead, but don't plan on napping to long if you know what I mean."

As Gena watched Sawn walk up the stairs, she thought to herself, "now me and Paula can finish what we started."

Paula bumped into Shawn at the top of the stairs. "What's up Shawn? You look tired," she said smiling.

"Yeahhh I'm a little beat, how you feeling?" He asked smiling.

"I feel great, fix'n to go down here and watch a little television," she said heading down the stairs.

Paula sat next to Gena saying, "Shawn just told me he was tired. What did you put in his food?"

Gena smiled saying, "I'm glad he's going to sleep. Now I can give you some of this," Gena stuck her tongue out.

After the two of them were done getting each other off, Gena sighed saying, "Paula you make me feel better than any man I ever known. I love you so...much!"

"Do you really?!"

"You know I do and by the way, we are going shopping tomorrow."

"When you say "we" do you mean me too?"

"Yes Paula, I mean you too so goin get you some sleep. I'll see you in the morning."

When Gena got upstairs to the bedroom she said to herself, "good he's still knocked out. I don't need dick tonight anyway. There's always another day, after all Paula was pleasing enough."

Gena climbed in the bed as quietly as she could trying not to wake Shawn and Shawn didn't move a muscle.

Gena lied down and fell into a deep dream, dreaming about her late husband. "Antonio why do you come home so drunk all the time?" She asked. "Why you lay in bed with all your clothes on?" Antonio asked. "I been waiting for your drunk ass to come home," she said. "Look at you, you been fucking with that dope all day you stupid bitch," Antonio snatched her up from the bed by her hair smiling. "You ain't shit," his hand met her face with a sudden blow. "Why can't you leave that shit alone? You no good for me." Throwing her on the floor, "I should blow your fucking brains out," he pointed his forty-five at her head. "No Antonio, please don't kill me!" The trigger slowly comes back, Gena screamed out, "noooo!" Before Antonio could release the trigger Gena woke up screaming "noooo!"

Shawn jumped up saying, "are you okay?" He said looking at the terror on her face.

I'm okay, I just had a bad dream that's all. Go back to sleep I'll be fine."

Thursday April 25, 1973 8:30 A.M.

Paula and Gena was the first to awake. They ran into each in the bathroom and decided to take their shower together. While they were showering, Shawn was awakened by the baby crying and said to himself, "where is Gena and Paula? I know they hear this baby crying. Hold on lil-man daddy coming." Shawn could hear the water running in the bathroom so he walked to see about the baby. "Come on lil-man, I guess your mother is in the shower." Shawn picked the baby up and headed out the room. He looked at the baby, "I'll be damned, their in the shower together. I'm starting to wonder about those two. Now when you get grown don't you go getting in the shower with your best friend. Come on let's go find us something to drink. A milk for you and a coffee for me sounds good huh?" He said walking down the stairs.

Later on that day at 1:00 P.M. Shawn took the girls out to Fairlane Mall. In the meantime, Alvin pulled in front of Dino's house and said, "good I see the rent-a-car."

Alvin parked saying, "damn, that's not the same color rent-a-car. That nigga done switched the rent-a-car from red to blue; even got the nerve to change the rims. That boy's crazy, I guess you do have a car," he said smiling.

Alvin pushed the doorbell; Dino's mom came to the door. "Alvin boy, is that you? Boy come on in here and let me look at you. You still the same with them pretty brown eyes," she said smiling.

"How you been doing Mrs. Brown?"

"I been fine, Dino is downstairs. I know he goin be glad to see you. Gone on down." Alvin walked away, "Lord these kids grow up so fast now'an days."

Dino was sitting downstairs at the big wooden table counting money and bagging dope. Alvin smiled saying, "how much you got there?"

Dino was surprised to see Alvin and said smiling, "what's up my brother? I know mama gave you one of her long lectures."

"N'all not this time."

"So what brings you this way my brother?" He said bagging the last sack.

"I thought I would drop by and see if you had everything under control for tonight."

"You know me man; I'm always on my job as you can see."

"Man that's chump change. I told you man, once we pull this little chicken scratch job off, I'm goin put you up on something much bigger than this lil kibbles and bits you messing with my brother. As a matter of fact grab that lil-shit and come with me."

"All of it?"

"Yeah all of it."

Dino put all the dope in a brown paper bag and followed Alvin up the basement stairs to the side door. Dino hollered out, "I'll be back in'ah minute mama."

"She didn't hear you man."

"Oh she heard me, you know mama, she's probably praying right now."

"Man she still pray every hour on the hour."

"Yepp, that's mama."

"When Dino and Alvin got in the car Alvin said, "now when we get up here on Visger Road I want you to take that lil-dope and pass it out for free to every crack-head we see from here to Bassett Street. Don't worry about the dope; roll the window down there go old Flip."

Dino rolled the window down and hollered out, "hey Flip!" Flip came to the car. "Here nigga don't say I ain't never given you nothing."

"Thanks Dino man," Flip said taking the pack of dope from Dino's hand.

"Let everybody know I got plenty of this shit."

Alvin smiled saying, "from this day on out Dino Southwest Detroit belong to you my brother."

Alvin and Dino rode up and down Visger Road passing out dope until they ran out.

"Well Alvin man, all the dope is gone, what now?"

After tomorrow lil-brother, I'm goin give you two million dollars worth of that shit. You can do whatever you want with it, and with a posse like yours you'll get rich overnight. I know you can run Southwest Detroit, and when you run out of yae-o you will cop from me and me only."

"What if I decided to cop from somebody else?"

"You won't, I know you, and why I know you won't cop from somebody else is because I'm connected with the top man himself and he get this shit straight out of Columbia. So sooner or later every nigga in the state of Michigan goin have to deal with Alvin Stone, and as long as you stay loyal to me, I'll make you the richest nigga in Southwest Detroit!"

"That sounds good to my ears man."

"Yeah I see you got'ah new paint job on your car. You don't waste no time do you?" Alvin said smiling.

"In this world you can't afford to waste time."

"After tomorrow you'll be able to afford anything you want in this world that I guarantee. Now when you get inside tell you mama that I said I love her, and don't forget to say a prayer for me, and remember Dino nine o'clock."

"We'll be there, you take care of yourself man."

"Later," Alvin said driving off.

After Shawn and his family were done shopping, they laughed and talked as they headed back towards the car holding their bags. Then all of a sudden, a blue van with six black gang members stared at them and stopped the van.

One of the men yelled you, "hey you sister, what you doing with them honkies? A queen like you looks too good to be standing next to some white bitch." Another one started talking, "what's the matter you whities ain't got no white friends?" Another one of the men started talking, "say white girl, I bet you wish you had a man like me; yoe punk ass boyfriend here ain't putting nothing in that pretty white ass."

Shawn went into a rage, "this is my wife you fucking with; you wanna fuck with somebody?" Shawn dropped his bags. "Fuck with me, don't none of you motha-fuckaz scare me. I'm not scared to die for mines."

Four security guards came to the scene. One of them asked, "what's the problem fellas?"

Shawn picked his bags up saying, "ain't no problem; these punks ready to die that's all. If I ever see y'all again I swear y'all dead meat, and I don't forget faces!"

Two of the security guards escorted Shawn to his car with Gena and Paula leading the way. Shawn opened the hatch as he threw the bags down. When he got in the car he said, "I wish I had my gun; I would'uv killed all they ass. From now on out I'm not leaving home without one. If I have to keep it in the glove compartment, that's where it's goin be. It's too damn dangerous out here without a gun!"

Gena put her head on Shawn's shoulder and said, "please Shawn, don't talk like that. Calm down, it's over now, we all are okay. Forget about it, let's go home!"

While Shawn drove, it was silent until Paula said, "come on you guys, ain't no need for us to act like this. I

don't know bout you two, but I could use a bite to eat. So
what will it be, pizza or burgers?"

"They both sound good to me," Shawn said getting
off the expressway.

They all agreed on pizza, and Shawn took them
straight to Little Caesar's where they sat for the next hour
and a half eating.

(Thursday night 8:50 P.M)

Alvin parked his car at the front entrance of the
warehouse, and waited inside his car for Dino to show up.
Alvin checked his watch for the third time, and said to
himself, "damn, it's eight-fifty, where the hell is Dino?"
Looking in his rearview mirror he spotted a bunch of
headlights coming his way. "Damn that got to be Dino and
his gangsters." The cars got closer. "Yeah that's them."

Alvin got out the car and sat on the hood of the car
and watched them as they parked their cars. Out of the
three cars Dino was the only one who got out. The rest of
the men stayed in their cars waiting on the signal from their
leader.

Dino walked up to Alvin and said, "what's up my
brother, we here."

"What's up with your men?"

"They want budge unless I give them a sign too."

"What you mean the sign?"

"Yeahhh that's right my brother; my men are trained better than a military man. Watch this my brother." Dino put his left hand on his chest and all the doors came open at the same time. Each man stood at attention and Dino smiled. "You like that don't you? Now watch this here." Dino took his left hand from his chest slowly bringing his right arm up and held it in the air spreading all five fingers.

Alvin watched the eleven men walk towards them and said, "damn Dino, I didn't know you was laying like this."

When they reached Dino, Dino said, "this my brother Alvin; he'll tell y'all mission when we get inside. Let's do this my brothers."

Once they got inside the warehouse Alvin did all the talking. "Men, now all of you know why y'all are here tonight. Now I'm goin keep it real with y'all; we may have to waste a few pigs, but what the fuck, we got to do what we got to do. This is a job brothers' and believe me, all of you will be well paid for your time and duty. I have every kind of weapon y'all can think of. I want each of you to grab a weapon that you know you can handle the best, cause tonight the first precinct is coming down. We goin blow that motha-fucka off the map."

One of the men said, "I can't wait I always did wanna blow that bitch up!"

Alvin smiled saying, "well you'll get that chance tonight. Now if anybody wants out, now is the time. You better speak up now cause once we get started ain't no turning back." Nobody spoke a word. "I guess that covers everything men grab all the artillery you want, and one more thing, I hope I don't have to stumble over none of you fellaz so do be careful. And when you shoot, shoot to kill! Now let's go to war!"

While the men were busy grabbing their artillery, Alvin was curious to see what was behind the other garage door. He slid the door back and said, "well, I just be damned, an Army truck, and look'ah here, the key already in the ignition. Bomoski you knew just what we needed."Alvin got inside the truck; it started right up. He cut it off and went to the back of it and raised the sliding door up. "I'll be damned fatigues. Dino bring your men over here. I want everybody to put on a camouflage hook up, we're in the Marines. Now I know why this Army swat truck is here, and I know why this Army shit is here. Dino you know it's a recruiting office in the next block from the police station; we goin park this baby right there. They'll think we just coming from the recruiting office if they see us coming. We can't lose, we too damn smooth. Y'all put some of that war paint on y'all faces, its war time."

After everybody was done changing into their army fatigues, Alvin said, "men, Ecorse Gangsters, let's do this shit, load up."

Alvin drove the Army truck and Dino sat on the passenger side. They didn't have that far to go being that they were already downtown.

Alvin looked over at Dino and said, "I don't know how long it's goin take this building to come down, but I know we got everything we need to get the job done. You ready my men?"

"Hell yeah, more than ever. You know you never did tell me why you were doing this?"

245

"Dino my brother, some things aren't meant to be told. Always remember this; the less people talk in this type of business, the longer they live!"

"I can dig that, I remember this nigga name Dale; he was at the pool room with me one day. Boy was winning his ass off this particular day; he was playing against the crack-man. Dale said, "damn nigga you ain't racking them balls tight enough." The rack man was already mad as hell from losing all four games to Dale' already so Dale just kept on running his mouth. "O stupid ass nigga, you win a game you sorry ass want have to rack." Rack-man said, "why I got to be stupid nigga?!" Dale said, "cause I called you stupid." Rack-man said, "boy you goin learn how to talk to me; I don't call you nothing, but what you name is, and I'll be damned if I'm goin stand here and let you call me everything, but Bill!" Dale looked in his eyes and said," whatever, you still a stupid motha-fucka." Everybody in the pool room was laughing at the way Dale was talking to the rack-man until the rack-man pulled put this little twenty-five automatic. The whole pool room got quiet as hell. Dale was still smiling until he saw that the rack-man wasn't joking. Rack-man said, "nigga I'll blow that grin off yoe face. I'll kill you nigga, lil-bitch ass nigga!" Dale said, "see now you wanna call me a bitch; if I was you I wouldn't pull'ah gun out unless I was goin use it bitch!" Rack-man said, "bitch…." And pointed the gun at Dale's head saying, "nigga, I'm goin teach you a lesson!" Dale said, "Please man," and slowly took a Kool cigarette out his shirt pocket and put it in his mouth. "I was looking, saying to myself, damn my man fix'n to kill Dale ass. Dale started trembling and saying, "please Bill man, don't do this man!" Rack-man started walking up on Dale with the gun pointed right at Dale's head saying, "n'all bitch, you gonna call me everything, but my name." The cigarette was shaking like hell in Dale's mouth. Rack-man said, "say goodbye to the world asshole!" And pulled the trigger. "All I heard was a click. Both of them niggas bust out laughing real loud. Damn gun was'ah cigarette lighter. After all the niggas in there started clapping, come to find out they pulled that lil-stunt almost once a month. I bet you thought rack-man was goin kill-em didn't you?"

"Nope, I saw that same stunt so many times. It fucked my mind up to the first time I saw it done. What we bout to do ain't no stunt; this the real thang, and I know I don't have to worry about you doing too much talking. I trust you, I know you down for yours."

"So are my man, they down too. If they wasn't down, they wouldn't be here tonight!"

"Oh I know they down, but we can't afford no slip ups. This job is important for you and me because if we don't succeed we don't get paid, and a man like me gots to have mine. What time is it?"

"Five minutes to ten."

"Good right on time. I want you to stick close to me. Anything happen to you, I don't know what I'll tell your mother. Knock on the window and tell yoe men to get ready. I'm about to park this baby."

Alvin parked the truck right on the corner from the precinct, and after he got all the men out the truck he gave them all a post saying, "I want a man on all four corners. You, you, you, and you I want you to two to make sure nobody comes out that jail. You two, I want y'all to place bombs everywhere you can in the building, and set the timer for ten minutes. That'll give them enough time to get

247

out. Dino our job is to take out everything moving at the desk. We don't have all night and move quickly. When y'all see us, come out the building, roll out. Now let's do this shit!"

The cameras in the police station had already focused in on them, but thought it was a regular military routine coming from the recruiting office in the next block over from them.

All the men went to their post that was assigned to them, and as Alvin and his men got closer to their destination, they were met by two police officers just getting off duty. One of the officers said, "good-night soldiers."

"Not for you two motha=fuckaz," Alvin said letting his oozie machine gun do the talking as the bullets made their way to the officers chests and heads. Alvin smiled, "don't worry, dead men can't talk, now quick, let's get this shit over with!"

Alvin and Dino rushed through the door firing shots after shots at everything that moved. Polices were coming from everywhere; Alvin and Dino stood chopping them down like trees until one of Dino's men ran up saying, "all the bombs is paced."

Alvin looked at his watch saying, "we have about seven minutes, fall out, it's time to ride."

As they were coming out the building a police car was pulling up, but two men that stood guarding the front of the jail that sat across from the police station never gave them a chance to get out the vehicle as they let their machine guns loose, killing the two officers instantly.

When the men "Gangsters" saw Alvin and Dino come running out the building, they ran behind them knowing their mission was completed.

Alvin drove off saying, "we did it y'all. In about three minutes we goin see more fireworks than on the fourth of July. I got to hand it to you Dino, yoe men did good, I like that!"

Dino smiled saying, "man I didn't know you was so cold-hearted."

"Well you know now, and as soon as I get my pay tomorrow I'll be to holla at'cha cause I don't want you to come after me with that crew you got."

"I wouldn't do that to you we brothers. I trust you with my life, if I didn't I wouldn't be here tonight with yoe crazy ass!"

"I know man, I could'nah pulled this shit off without you, I owe you big time."

Alvin pulled over about a half mile away from the precinct and said, "watch this shit." In about thirty seconds all they could see and hear was boom, boom, boom. Smoke and fire covered the air. Alvin just smiled telling Dino, "happy fourth of July."

Alvin pulled off taking the men back to their cars. Everybody got in their cars going their own separate way.

Meanwhile, Shawn and Gena along with Paula were sitting in the living room watching the Johnny Carson show when the program was interrupted by channel 11 news.

"We interrupt this program to bring you this channel eleven news update. As you can see, fire fighters are working hard to bring the dead bodies from what use to be a police station; so far twelve brutally burned bodies have been found. Four officers were found outside of the station crucially shot to death. It is said that a gang of men is responsible for tonight's action. It's still not clear how many people died in this tragedy tonight. No one has been arrested so far. I'll have more news on our bombing that killed many here tonight. I'm Jack Denning, channel 11 news."

Shawn thought to himself, "my man Alvin Stone. Now I don't have to worry about the photos or the tape. I'll see you tomorrow Alvin. I knew you could do it; knew you could pull it off. I just wish I was there to see that sucka fall to the ground."

Gena just shook her head and said, "that's a shame all them people got killed, and it's really a shame the police ain't even safe at their own police station. I'm glad we got you out of there honey; I wouldn't know what I would do without you!"

Shawn stood up to leave saying, "they should'uv killed they ass, I can't stand cops!"

"You shouldn't talk like that, those cops are humans too!"

"I can't help it Gena, I hate cops!"

"Where you fix'n to go?"

"To bed, if you don't mind."

"I didn't mean to upset you; hold up, I'm coming too."

Paula said, "oh y'all just goin leave me, huh?"

Gena smiled anyway, "we'll see you in the morning."

"Well good night to y'all too."

Gena and Shawn went upstairs and got undressed. Both of them got in the bed at the same time. Gena said, "you not mad at me are you?"

"No sweetheart, I'm not mad at all."

"Good," she said going under the sheet placing her mouth on his cock.

Shawn threw the sheet back saying, "yeah baby, damn you feel so good."

Gena stopped sucking for a second and said, "oh do I? Well I want you do something to me you never done before."

"And what's that baby?"

"I want you to fuck me in my ass until you come inside of me."

"Hold on, I better get some grease."

Shawn rubbed the Vaseline all over his penis, and gently stuck the tip of his dickhead in Gena's round eye. When the head of Shawn's cock entered her she screamed out, "oh yes Shawn, go deeper." Shawn went a little deeper. "Oooh yeah, go slow Shawn, yes, yes, yes, give it to me Shawn."

Shawn penetrated and rolled to the side, sighing in relief saying, "I love you Gena."

Gena spread her legs wide open, letting Shawn's eyes stare into the wetness of her cunt saying, "I love you too Shawn, make love to me, I want you now."

Paula was standing outside their door listening with one ear against the door, and the other hand moving in and out her cunt. As she continued to listen to Gena cry out in passion, she said to herself, "damn I wish I was in her shoes right about now." Paula started cumming after hearing Gena saying, "oh yeah Shawn, fuck me, fuck me, I'm cumming, I'm cumming, yes Shawn." Paula's mind was telling her to goin the room, but she couldn't build up the nerves. "If Shawn would come out that room right now, I'll let'em fuck me, and it wouldn't even cost him a dime this time. Damn my pussy is on fire, I need me a man. They finally done stopped, guess I'll take my wet ass to sleep now. Tomorrow I'm goin find me'ah man so he can screw my brains out. Men, you can't live with them, you can't live without them. Goodnight you two love birds," she said walking away from their bedroom door.

Friday April 25, 1973 1:00 P.M.

Shawn's beeper started vibrating, and Shawn said to himself, "damn this got to be Alvin, let me call his ass. I don't want no shit out of him." Shawn dialed the number and Alvin answered the phone, "hello."

"Alvin my main man, you have done well. I want you to meet me at the Northwest Storage at two-thirty. Do you know how to get there?"

"You bet I do. Now how I know you ain't leading me into no ambush?"

"Like you Stone, my word is also my bond."

"That's what I'm talking about Bomoski, see you at two-thirty." Alvin hung the phone up and smiled saying out loud to himself, "yeah Bomoski, I know you are a man of your word. Let me get my black ass out'uv this phone booth and order me a Budweiser," He came out the phone booth and yelled out, "hey Peggy, one bud please."

When she handed Alvin the beer, he chugged it down and said, "you have a nice day Peggy."

"You too Alvin," she said smiling. "Thanks for the tip."

"Anything for you baby," he said walking out the bar.

Peggy smiled and said to herself, "I been trying to give that boy some of this pussy for twelve years now, and he still want give me no play. One of these good old days that brown eye lover goin get wit this."

253

Alvin cruised around in the neighborhood killing time. He looked at his Rolex watch and said, "it's two-fifteen." He got on I-96 and drove straight to Northwest Storage.

When Alvin arrived, Shawn was already there. Alvin parked his car next to Shawn's car, and got out and checked is windshield wiper.

Shawn walked up to Alvin and shook his hand saying, "Alvin Stone, today you become a rich man; job well done!"

Alvin smiled and said, "I hope to get like you Bomoski, powerful."

"Well you definitely have the right stuff to do it with, and plus you have the heart. I hope the best for you my friend, come with me."

When they got inside the storage room Shawn said, "these two storage bas right here are yours, and this is the brief case you'll find eleven hundred thousand. I want you to make sure your man get paid swell for their time."
"I thought you were goin leave them up to me to pay out my pockets."

"When I send a man on a mission, I make sure I take care all who he hires. That's the way the business is run."

"I didn't know that."

"Well you do now. We better be going our separate ways before somebody come."

"I'll stay in touch with you Bomoski."

"I know you will, take care Alvin."

"I still can't believe you paying all the hired help, but it's all good. Take care Bomoski, I'm fix'n to go and get the show on the road."

Alvin put the money and dope in the backseat of the car saying to himself, "all I got'ah do now is pay Dino and his boys off. Dino probably got his ass home at home waiting for me to show up. I made him pass all his dope out too."

Fifty minutes later Alvin was knocking on Dino's side door trying to avoid Dino's mother. Dino was down in the basement and could hear the soft taps on the side door. He quickly ran up the basement stairs and looked out the window to see who was knocking. A smile came across his face when he saw that it was Alvin.

"Come on in man, I was just thinking about yoe ass."

Alvin smiled saying, "oh yeah, I hope it was all good lil-brother."

"You know me man, I always think good thoughts about you my brother. What's in the brief case?"

"A little bonus for you and your men. I want you to split this up with them. It's eleven hundred thousand. Now for you, I got the, your hook up in my car. I want you to take it easy; don't start selling so much so quick. Take your time; work your way into the groove of things that way you want ever have to worry about getting busted, cause we got plenty of that shit man. I mean plenty."

"Hey whatever you say man, you know the dope game better than me. I'm just'ah rookie compared to you."

"I didn't wanna bring the dope in right away; your mother might'uv came to the door. I'll run and get it real quick."

"I'm glad you be thinking man. You know how my mama is, wanna know what's in every bag she see coming through the door."

"Yeahhh that's your mama, she'll never change. I guess that's why I have so much respect for her. She believes in doing the right things in life. I'll be right back man, let me go get this shit out the car. Stay by the door, cause I'm out'uv here when I give you yoe share."

Alvin ran to his car and grabbed the dope and ran back to Dino saying, "be careful man. I love you man and once again I thank you for coming through for me!"

Dino gave Alvin the high-five, and said, "anytime for you my brother. You take it easy yoe-self out there, I'll be in touch." Dino watched Alvin get into his car. "That boy sure do keep that car shining like new money.

As Alvin cruised down Visger Road looking at all the drug addicts he said to himself, "from now on its kilos only for me. I'm not selling nothing under that. I'm fix'n to live like a king; look out Detroit, Alvin Stone is back."